THE HIDDEN YEARS

JOHN OXENHAM'S NOVELS

GOD'S PRISONER.
RISING FORTUNES.
OUR LADY OF DELIVERANCE.
A PRINCESS OF VASCOVY.
JOHN OF GERISAU.
UNDER THE IRON FLAIL.
BONDMAN FREE.
MR. JOSEPH SCORER.
BARBE OF GRAND BAYOU.
A WEAVER OF WEBS.
HEARTS IN EXILE.
THE GATE OF THE DESERT.
WHITE FIRE.
GIANT CIRCUMSTANCE.
PROFIT AND LOSS.
THE LONG ROAD.
CARETTE OF SARK.
PEARL OF PEARL ISLAND.
THE SONG OF HYACINTH.
MY LADY OF SHADOWS.
GREAT-HEART GILLIAN.
A MAID OF THE SILVER SEA.

LAURISTONS.
THE COIL OF CARNE.
THEIR HIGH ADVENTURE.
QUEEN OF THE GUARDED MOUNTS.
MR. CHERRY RETIRED ? !
THE QUEST OF THE GOLDEN ROSE.
MARY ALL-ALONE.
RED WRATH.
MAID OF THE MIST.
BROKEN SHACKLES.
FLOWER OF THE DUST.
MY LADY OF THE MOOR.
" 1914."
THE LOOSING OF THE LION'S WHELPS.
CORNER ISLAND.
A HAZARD IN THE BLUE.
THE PERILOUS LOVERS.
CHAPERON TO CUPID.
SCALA SANCTA.
THE RECOLLECTIONS OF RODERIC FYFE.
THE HAWK OF COMO.
LAKE OF DREAMS.

DIVERSE

BEES IN AMBER.
" ALL'S WELL ! "
THE KING'S HIGH WAY.
THE VISION SPLENDID.
THE FIERY CROSS.
HIGH ALTARS.
HEARTS COURAGEOUS.
" ALL CLEAR ! "
WINDS OF THE DAWN.
A LITTLE TE DEUM.
THE LATER TE DEUMS.
THE SACRAMENTS.
HYMN FOR THE MEN AT THE FRONT.
WIDE HORIZONS.
CHAOS—AND THE WAY OUT.
" GENTLEMEN !—THE KING."
THE WONDER OF LOURDES.
THE CEDAR BOX.
SELECTED POEMS.
THE HIDDEN YEARS.
THE MAN WHO WOULD SAVE THE WORLD.
GOD'S CANDLE.
THE SPLENDOUR OF THE DAWN.
CROSS ROADS.
A SAINT IN THE MAKING.
ANNO DOMINI.
GOD AND LADY MARGARET.
CHRIST AND THE THIRD WISE MAN.
OUT OF THE BODY.

" J.O." (Biography) by ERICA OXENHAM.
SCRAP BOOK OF J.O. by ERICA OXENHAM.

THE HIDDEN YEARS

BY

JOHN OXENHAM

DAVID McKAY COMPANY, INC.
New York

IN
MEMORY
OF
HIM

CONTENTS

CHAPTER   PAGE

1 Tells of my Meeting with the Boy   .   1

2 Of the Beginnings of a Great Friendship   9

3 Of Hero-Worship.   24

4 Of the Coming of Tobias   .   .   .   31

5 Of the Hills, the Pool and the Great
   Road   36

6 Of the Right Making of Yokes   .   .   44

7 Of his Ways with "The Family".   .   53

8 Of our Meeting with Cousin John   .   59

9 Of his Heights and Depths and Breadths   69

10 Of my Quest after two Fair Maids   .   77

11 Of our Treasure-Trove   87

12 Of Noble Lovers   92

13 Of his Ways with Men   .   .   .   101

14 Of his Grief at the Loss of his Friend   108

15 Of a Fight he Fought and Won .   .   111

16 Of the Making of the Seamless Robe   .   118

17 Of the Coming of the Cousins   .   .   123

18 Of the Move to the Lake   .   .   .   131

19 Of the Coming of Little John   .   .   138

20 Of the New Prophet   143

CONTENTS

CHAPTER		PAGE
21	Of an Unexpected Visit	149
22	Of a Greater Prophet still	156
23	Of his Coming to his Own	161
24	Of the Return of Arni	167
25	Of his Rejection by his Own	176
26	Of our Journey through the Valley of Shadows	188
27	Of the Tumultuous City	194
28	Of a Rest Without while the Storm brewed Within	201
29	Of Life and Death at the Prætorium	205
30	Of the Way of Sorrowful Triumph	213
31	Of the Baring of Zerah's Heart	221
32	Of the Wonderful Visit	232
33	Of the Long Days since	240

THE HIDDEN YEARS

THE HIDDEN YEARS

CHAPTER I

Tells of my Meeting with the Boy

My father was a boat-builder at Ptolemais, the
Galilean port on the western coast, through which
came most of the goods for and from Damascus
and the desert.

He was a skilled craftsman and there were no
better boats along all that shore than the ones he
built.   But he was a man of advanced ideas and
was always trying new styles in boats, some of
which were improvements and some dangerous.

It was in testing one of these last that he lost
his life when I was about nine years old.   And my
mother, hating the sea because it had bereaved
her, decided to return to her native village among
the hills of Galilee.

With all our belongings piled on an ox-cart the
journey took us the best part of two days.   We
reached Nazaret just before sundown on the
second day and went to the house of my mother's
brother till we should find one for ourselves.   He
was Joda ben Ahaz, the village mason, and was

in a good way of business, and he gave us warm welcome.

He knew, of course, every house in the village, and when my mother asked his advice as to one for us to live in, he said at once, " There is a little house up on the hill there, next door to Joseph ben Heli's, the carpenter. Old Eleazer, the Teacher, lived there and it has been empty ever since he died. It is small but you are only two. And it is well built, for I built it myself, and I dug right down to the rock to be sure of its foundations. And you will have good neighbours, not like some of the others. Joseph and his wife, Mary, are held in great esteem. They are of the line of David, you see, and they have travelled and seen the world. He is a good workman and learned all he could when he was in Egypt and it has stood him in good stead. No one hereabouts makes such chests and chairs as he does."

" We will look at the house to-morrow," said my mother.

And that was how we came to live next door to Joseph the Carpenter and his wife Mary.

The little house needed some repairs and alterations, and my mother went at once to Joseph's workshop to tell him what she wanted done.

I remember it so well. The workshop was at the side of the house looking down over the rest of the village, and one side of it was all open to the air and sunshine.

Joseph was hard at work. We could hear his plane going 'seep-seep-seep' as we drew near. There was a boy with him. He was older than myself and a good head taller.

Uncle Joda had not said anything about there being a boy. But I was glad there was one, and not too old for me to get to know. For at Ptolemais my mother would not have me go much with the boys of the port, they were so rough and uncouth through mixing with the sailors from all over the world.

So I looked at this boy eagerly and wondered if we were likely to be friends. It would make such a difference to me.

The boy was the first to see us coming. He said a word to his father, and the seep-seep of the plane stopped and Joseph came out to greet us, the boy with him.

Joseph seemed to me quite an old man. His hair and beard were beginning to go gray. His eyes were deep under bushy brows, but his face was kindly.

He looked intently at my mother and then said, " You must be Miriam, the daughter of Eliakim. I remember being at your wedding. You married Azor of Ptolemais, the boat-builder."

" Yes," she said quietly. " He was drowned five weeks ago and I have come back home to Nazaret to live—in that house that was Eleazer's."

" It is better than Ptolemais for a lone woman. They are rough folk there."

"Yes. And since the sea took my man I hate the sight of it."

"And this is your son?"

"My son Azor. My only one. I did not want him to grow up to the sea. . . . And this is yours?"

"Our little Jesus," Joseph said quietly, and put his brown hairy hand lovingly on the boy's shoulder.

My mother looked very intently at the boy, and I liked him at once for the frank, happy way in which he looked back at her and then at me as if he wanted to be friends.

His hair was brown, but, where the sun caught it, it looked almost like gold or bronze. And his eyes were brown also, and there was something in them that caused me joy though I could not tell what. They were not deep under bushy brows like his father's, and yet, somehow, they seemed to me deep eyes—very seeing eyes. For there are deep eyes and shallow eyes, and experience has taught me that deep eyes see most. This boy's eyes were deep ones and there was a little spark in each, like a star.

"I hope they will be friends," said my mother, looking from him to me.

"They will be friends," said Joseph quietly. "Jesus is friends with them all. What is he going to be—yours?" with a nod towards me.

"A carpenter," I said boldly, before she could answer.

"He was to have followed his father," said my

mother. " He was always in the yard among the boats. But now——"

" There's plenty to do besides building boats. And if he loves wood——"

" Yes," I said, " I love wood—all kinds of wood—and tools."

" He will be a carpenter," said Joseph, with a grave smile. " It won't make him rich but he will find joy in good work. Come along in and see Mary, and we will talk over what you want done to the house," and he led her in through the workshop, leaving me and the boy together.

He came up to me and put his arm over my shoulder saying, " You love wood and I love wood—and the handling of it. But, do you know, Little Azor . . . I wonder sometimes if it does not perhaps hurt it—the saw and the plane and the chisel going into it."

" Hurt it ? "—I stopped in our course to the workshop and stood and stared at him. " But how can it hurt it ? It's only wood."

" But it had life in it until it was cut down, and anything that has life in it can feel."

" But if trees were never cut down we would have no wood for doors and boxes and things."

" And no carpenters," he smiled. " But if it feels, maybe it is pleased to be put to better service than just growing. We'll hope so. . . . What tools do you know ? "

" I know them all, but I can't use them all properly yet."

" Can you dovetail ? "

" No, I never learnt that. We didn't do it in our boats, or very little. Can you ? "

" See !—my father taught me. It's fine. But it's not easy. You've got to get it so exact. But when you do get it right. . . ." And he drew out from under a bundle of shavings below the bench a wooden box—cedar and very sweet-smelling—and held it towards me.

" Did you do it ? . . . all yourself ? "

" Every little bit of it. It took a long time but it's about done now," and he ran his slim brown fingers along its sides ; and in a whisper, with a finger on his lip, he said, " It's for my mother on her birthday, and that's two days from to-day."

His questing fingers thought they detected a slight unevenness in one of its sides, and he picked up a chisel and ran it gently along to smooth it out.

" You see, it's got to be perfect because it's for her," he said, with a gleaming glance at me. And, because of that, the chisel ran into his finger and set it bleeding.

The bright red blood dripped down on to the shavings. He looked at it for a moment and then put it into his mouth and sucked it.

" That comes of not looking what I was doing," he laughed. " But in this hot weather it will do no harm to lose a little blood. Old Eleazer used to tell us that in the Law all things are made holier by the letting of blood."

He went thoughtful for a moment and then nodded his head and said, " Yes, I'm glad I cut my finger, Little Azor. It's as though I had shed some blood for my mother . . . though truly "— with a merry laugh—" it was my own carelessness that did it."

Then, from a little cupboard on a shelf, he got out a bit of linen rag and twisted it round and round and made me tie it tight, saying :

" It will be all right in a day or two. I always heal up quickly. And it won't stop me helping with your house either. I'm glad you are coming next door. We shall be good friends."

I remember every word he said, that first day I met him, as indeed I have remembered almost all that I ever heard him say. For he captured my heart.

He seemed to me the very splendidest boy I had ever met. But I had not met many, and not one I had ever felt I could be such friends with as I could with this boy. And I was glad.

When Joseph came out with our two mothers we all went along to our house to point out what needed to be done to it.

And the boy's mother put her two hands on my shoulders and looked down at me and said, " And this is your son, Miriam !—he's a bright-looking little fellow. They will make good friends, these two. You will be glad to have him away from Ptolemais."

" Yes, truly," said my mother. " It's no place for boys."

" How old is he ? "

" Well, he's just on nine—though he doesn't

look it, I know.   Perhaps he'll begin to grow on
the hills here."

The boy's mother was younger, I thought, than
mine, and almost as beautiful—very sweet of face
and very gentle in her manner ; and her eyes,
like the boy's, had strange deeps in them.   They
drew you.   And now—thinking back on it all—
I know that there was in them a constant look of
wonder, and perhaps somewhat of apprehension.

CHAPTER II

OF THE BEGINNINGS OF A GREAT FRIENDSHIP

JOSEPH and the boy worked at our house for three days, putting up shelves and cupboards and arranging our things, and on the third day we went into it.

It was very much smaller than our house at Ptolemais, but it was big enough for the two of us and my mother was well pleased with it. For me, the joy of having that boy as neighbour would have more than made up for even a smaller house still.

I had worked with him and his father these three days, handing them tools and fetching and carrying, and the more I saw of him the more I liked him.

He was a clever little workman and so even-tempered that nothing ever put him out, not even when he once hit his thumb with a hammer a blow that made his eyes water. It was really my fault again; for I had asked him something and he had looked over his shoulder to answer me.

He made a little face at me for a moment, then rubbed the thumb violently and sucked it for a

time, and then went on with his work as gaily as
ever.

That first night I went up on to the roof with
my mother to watch the sun set between the hills
along the valley. There were hills all round,
but they fell back towards the east and west and
our house stood so high that we could see well
both ways and over the white houses of the
village.

Behind the house was our plot of land enclosed
by a rough stone wall. There were some vines
in it and two tall cypress-trees, and a wide-
spreading fig-tree full of big leaves and the little
knobs of coming figs.

"We can grow all we need," said my mother.
"But we shall have to work, little son. We are
but poor folk now."

"I will work hard, mother——" And then
we heard a joyous shout below, and saw Joseph's
boy bounding along the stony track that led past
his house and ours along the hillside.

"He is a beautiful boy," said my mother, as we
stood watching.

And beautiful he was, with the sunset gold
in his hair and his face all alight and his eyes
shining.

"Azor! Little Azor!" he cried, with a wave
of the arm. "Will you come with me to the
hill-top to-morrow to see the sun rise ? It is
wonderful——" He stood panting below us——
"We will take food and spend the day up there.
I am to have holiday because I've been working

so hard these three days. You will let him, mother ? " And it was not in my mother to say him nay.

" You will look after him, Jesus, and not let him get into any mischief ? "

" I never get anyone into any mischief, mother —never ! " he panted earnestly. " You will let him come ? "

" Yes, he shall come. I can trust him with you," and I danced on the roof with delight. " I will bake him some cakes to-night."

" An hour before the dawn then," and with a whoop and a wave he was off again.

" A beautiful boy ! " said my mother again, as we stood looking after him. " I hope you will grow up like him, my little Azor." And even that did not in the least lessen my liking for him.

I was up and waiting long before the time, with four cakes and some figs and some dates in a little linen bag over my shoulder, and anticipation in my heart which all the linen bags in the world could not have contained.

The moment I heard his footstep on the path I shot out to meet him. He flung his arm over my shoulder for a moment and we went on along the hill-track.

It was still dark, and the air was crisp and cool and full of the clean sweet smell of the earth and growing things.

" We will keep our breath for the hill," said the boy. " It's steep up there," and we went in silence along the shadowy path.

I could not see it, but I followed close on his heels. He went lightly and with a joyous spring and I did my best to do the same.

As we passed through an olive grove the birds began to twitter in the trees, with tiny rustlings.

" They are saying their morning prayers," said the boy softly. " Then they will fall asleep again. It is not time for them to get up yet."

I was panting heavily when at last we came out on the crest of the hill, but the boy, though he breathed deeply and quietly, showed no other sign of unusual exertion.

" You are not used to the hills, Little Azor," he said. " At Ptolemais you had none like ours."

" Carmel ! " I panted. " But too far away . . . across the sea."

" Lie you flat on your back there. You'll be all right before the sun comes. You must learn to climb with your mouth shut tight. See those little pink clouds up there. They can see him though we cannot. They are saying their prayers too."

He moved off towards the eastern side of the crest, and I lay flat and panted-in such great gulps of the sweet strong air that I felt as if I would burst or fly.

Then the little purple and pink clouds at which I was staring turned white, with crimson edges. They looked like myriads of little white angels with glowing wings. And the ground all about me was thick with flowers. Right above me a hawk hung motionless as though watching us.

I heard the boy singing. I sat up and saw him standing at the edge of the hill-top, with his face to the sun and his arms stretched high above his head—such a beautiful slim young thing! I can see him yet—lithe and brown, and graceful as an antelope. He had slipped his arms out of his meil, so that it had fallen and hung now like a kirtle round his waist, leaving all the top part of him bare and of a much lighter colour than the rest, for his face and neck and arms and legs were burned brown with the sun.

His hands seemed as though reaching up to heaven for a blessing—as though it were there waiting for him and he would drag it down.

And as I got up and went to him, this was what he was singing:

"Eloi! Eloi! Eloi!
Praise! Praise! Praise!
Praise to God for His fair morning light!
Praise for the Love that kept us through the night!
Praise for the Power that guides the world aright!
And Praise, Praise, Praise, for His good gift of sight!"

As I came alongside he threw an arm round my neck without turning or stopping his singing. And, I know not why, unless it was that in all things I wanted to be like him, I, too, loosed my arms and with a shake my tunic fell to my girdle, and I stood beside him bare like himself. A tighten-

ing of his arm round my neck showed me that he
was glad.

The sun had stolen silently above the eastern
hills as I came to him.   I caught the first glimmer
of the great round golden eye above a far-away
rocky crest, and as we stood there he rose, swiftly
and silently, and so full of majesty and beauty that
I was stricken with awe.   I had never watched
a sunrise like that before, for our house at
Ptolemais was on the shore and the hills and the
town rose up behind it.

" It is wonderful," I jerked, when the boy had
fallen silent, watching eagerly, his face all golden
in the sunlight.

" Yes—it is wonderful—always wonderful. . . .
' As a bridegroom coming out of his chamber
. . . rejoicing as a strong man to run a race ! ' "

" That's King David in the Book of Praise," I
said, proud of my knowledge.

" Do you ever thank God for your eyes, Little
Azor ? " he asked suddenly.

" I'm glad of them."

" Well, if you think of Him when you're glad
of them then you're thanking Him.   I thank
Him always for all that He has given me—the
big things and the little things.   And I thank
Him for myself and for all who may perhaps
sometimes forget to thank Him."

I had never seen any sight so wonderful as
the one from that hill-top, and presently the boy
told me the names of the places, and that made it
more wonderful still.   For the very names made

one's heart beat quicker, even though the tale of its beating ran to no more than nine short years.

"Those are the hills of Lebanon . . . and that white peak is Hermon—old Father Hermon. . . . The gleam over there is our great lake. You can just get a peep of it between the hills. . . . And there is Tabor . . . and Gilboa . . . and the Valley of Jezreel—Gideon and Saul and Jonathan, you know—and the hills of Samaria. And over there——"

"Carmel," I cried. "Our own Carmel—and the sea, and Ptolemais . . . though you can't see it."

"Oh, it is a beautiful land . . . a beautiful, beautiful land," he cried rapturously. "See all the villages below us . . . all full of people. . . . All—full—of—people"—he said it slowly and thoughtfully. And again—"Full—of—people; rich people and poor people; good people and—not so good people; happy people and sad people. . . ." And he stood gazing out over the world with wondering eyes.

Then, still full of thought, he pulled up his tunic and slipped it on, for the sun was getting hot; and he sat down and said, "Let us eat. You are hungry, Little Azor."

"Yes, I am hungry," and as we sat eating our cakes, when we had exchanged one each, and our dates and figs, I asked him,

"Why do you stand like that when you sing your prayers, Jesus?"

And he thought for a moment and then said,

" Face to face like that with Him I feel closer to Him . . . nothing between us. . . . Just me and Him."

And then he put his finger to his lip, for a number of little birds had alighted in the grass and flowers beside us and were hopping nearer and nearer.

They came right up to him and showed no fear. They hopped on to his legs, and cheeped happily and hungrily, and looked confidently up at him with their bright little beads of eyes.

He crumbled some bits of cake and fed them out of his hand. Their quick little eyes were like jewels, and they hopped and fluttered their wings as though they were thanking him. I would have liked them to come to me too, but they would not.

Then there was a sudden rush of wings above us, and the hawk I had seen watching us swooped down after a bird in the grass close by. The boy sprang up with a shout which made it swerve, and the bird escaped. And then he felt something fluttering in his breast, and he put in his hand and found two of the small birds fled in there for safety. He stroked them gently and soothed their fears.

" I love them," he said softly—" all little fearful things. And they all know it and have no fear of me. But the hawks—no, I do not like them. . . . And I cannot understand . . . for the hawks must live you see. . . . God made them too. . . . They are all of the family. . . .

No, I do not understand, Little Azor . . . sometime, maybe . . ." and he fell thoughtful over it.

The birds lay quietly in the fold of his tunic
above the girdle, as though they would like to
nest there.

" We will loose them in the grove down yonder,
and then they will feel safe," he said. . . . And
presently, " And one day we will go along to the
Great Road and watch the world pass by. You
have seen it all at Ptolemais, Little Azor, but to me
it is always a marvel, and I love to lie and watch
it. But to-day I would stop on the heights."

So we went down into the grove, but the birds
were very loth to leave him, and in the end he had
to make a little nest among the flowers. And
putting them into it he patted their heads gently
and bade them stay there, and we went on our
way.

" Don't you love all the little things, Little
Azor ? " he said, as we went on, with his arm warm
round my neck, down into the dip and up another
hill. " They are all little brothers and sisters to
me and I love to talk to them."

" I don't know them as you do, Jesus," I said
excusingly. " And they wouldn't come to me as
they do to you."

" It is just because I love them so much and I
think they know it. They are very clever little
people and perhaps they know more than we
suppose. If you truly love them they will soon
find it out. . . . Dogs now ! Most people
despise them, but to me they are dearer even than

the birds or the coneys or the baby foxes. Something in their eyes, I think it is. They understand. Sometimes I think they are really trying to speak to me. Souls of some kind I am sure they have or they could not look at one like that."

That whole long first day I spent with the boy among the hills is stamped upon my memory.

I was just at the age that craved a hero to worship, and this boy filled my need to the brim. Everything he did and everything he said was wonderful to me, and my whole small heart went out to him. For, you see, as I have said, the boys of Ptolemais were coarse and rude through mixing with men of all the nations of the earth, and I had never known anyone towards whom I felt as I did towards this boy.

And he was so good to look at—so strong and healthy and clean and wholesome—though that last word I would not have understood the meaning of at that time. But I have come to know since that it was just that wholeness and wholesomeness that drew me so to him.

When he ran down one hill and up the next he went like a mountain deer, so fleet and light and springy. And then when he sat on a rock up above and waved and hallooed to me, panting along down below, he was so good to look at, with his golden-brown hair blowing in the wind, and the bright little stars shining in his big brown eyes. And his voice when he called to me, " Well done, Little Azor, well done ! Keep it up ! You're nearly there "—his voice was like the trumpets of the Roman soldiers at Ptolemais, only very much sweeter.

Then I would struggle up to him—sitting there with his tunic flung over his shoulders—and fall flat by his side, and he would laugh and look down at me, and would say, " You'll soon get your wind all right and do it without panting like that. You're not in good condition yet, with living down there in Ptolemais. But our hills will soon cure that."

Rambling at large among the hills that day we came at last on the big pond in the hollow into which all the streams and springs up there drained. And at sight of it we broke into a run, for the sun was hot and the air in the basin was heavy.

We pulled off our tunics as we ran, and dashed into the water with a shout, and I flung myself forward on my face and struck straight out, for I could swim like a fish, thanks to my father's insistence. For he would not let me go out in a boat till I was sure of myself in the water.

And then, to my great surprise, for I had not supposed there was anything the boy could not do, and to my joy also at finding I could do something that he could not, I heard a shout behind me, and looking back, saw him standing there up to his chin, but venturing no further.

" Ho, Little Fish ! Come back and show me this ! Ptolemais taught you one good thing."

As I swam back he watched keenly every movement of my arms and legs. Then he settled himself in the water and struck out without any doubt or fear, and we swam side by side far out into the pond.

"Oh but this is good . . . good . . . good!" he cried, when I showed him how to turn on his back and float. "You see, we don't often come so far as this, and none of us could swim. We'll teach the others. They'll love it."

"They'll have to learn or they may get drowned."

"But it's as easy as running," he said. "Why should they get drowned?"

But, young as I was, I knew that his easy mastery of it came from his absolute lack of fear. It had taken me many days, and after that, many weeks, and I had had fears enough before I became at home in the water, but he, through knowing no fear, was a swimmer already.

We played about there for hours—running races round the pool and up and down the neighbouring slopes, and in those I had no chance against him.

But at the far side of the pool there stood a great willow-tree, with its feet in the water and some of its branches overhanging. And I got level with the boy by climbing out along one of these and diving down into the depths. That too he had to learn, and he was in and out and along the branch a dozen times before he was satisfied.

As he shook the water out of his eyes, the last time he came up—"Look there, Little Fish," he cried, "we are in for a wetting"—at which I

laughed, for we had been as wet as we could be
for hours.

But looking, I saw a great black cloud sweeping
in from the West and darkening all the sky.

" Will it thunder ? " I asked anxiously, for I
was still child enough to feel discomfort, if not
actual fear, when the heavens roared and rattled,
as I had heard them do round Carmel, when they
seemed to be trying their best to shatter it to
pieces.

" Yes, it will thunder and it will lighten, and
we are a long way from home, Little Azor. But
you are not afraid of the thunder ? "

" I d-don't like it," I chittered, as I got hastily
into my tunic, for the air seemed to have grown
colder and I felt suddenly naked and defenceless
against the weather.

So we set off home at a run, he holding me by
the hand and assuring me again and again that
there was nothing to be afraid of.

But I remembered the Roman galley that was
struck by lightning in Akka bay and sunk with all
its rowers chained to their benches. So I was not
much reassured, but his strong, warm hand was
comforting and I did my best to make myself
believe that I was not really afraid.

We kept along the valley till we had to strike up
to get across to Nazaret. And the thunder was
clapping all about us and rattling among the hills,
and rolling along the black sky towards the lake,
long before we began to climb the hill.

But the boy seemed actually to like it, for he

began singing at the top of his voice, though at times I could hardly hear him for the thunder and the rain.—

> " It is the Glory of God that thundereth . . .
>   Eloi! Eloi! Eloi!
>   The Voice of the Lord is powerful . . .
>   The Voice of the Lord is full of Majesty . . .
>   The Voice of the Lord shaketh the wilderness . . .
>   The Lord sitteth upon the flood . . .
>   Yea, the Lord sitteth King for ever . . .
>   Eloi! Eloi! Eloi! "

And whenever the lightning flamed out and tore a jagged rent in the black sky, and my sodden little hand would give a quiver in his, his warm hand would grip it still more tightly, and he would look down at me and smile. And that comforted me much.

If I had been caught like that alone I should just have lain down flat on the earth, and covered my head with my tunic, and waited till it passed. But the boy went steadily on, up and up the hill till we got to the top. And there I was panting so that we had to stop and I sank down into the wet grass.

I shall never forget that first day out with the boy in that great thunderstorm. After all these years I can close my eyes and see him standing there just as he had stood in the sunrise.

He had gone back a few paces to the edge of the hill, and he stood there as he had done then, with his arms thrown up towards the terrible black sky. He had slipped his tunic again,—it was, indeed, no more than a wet rag now,—and he stood there just as he had stood to welcome the sun. But now the rain thrashed over him, and when the lightning blazed in front he looked like a figure carved in shining black marble.

> " The Voice of the Lord shaketh the wilderness . . .
> The Lord sitteth upon the flood . . .
> Yea, the Lord sitteth King for ever . . .
> The Lord will give strength unto His people . . .
> The Lord will bless His people with peace . . ."

So he sang amid the thunder-claps, and his voice was as steady as a trumpet, and he knew no fear.

But for me, I lay small in the grass, and clasped my sodden tunic tight about me as protection against the thunder and the lightning.

CHAPTER III

OF HERO-WORSHIP

THE boys and girls of our village were very different from those of Ptolemais.

Jesus had left school before we came to live there, and the others said he knew as much of the Law and the Prophets and the Book of Praise as the Teacher did himself. For he was very quick at learning anything. He set his whole mind to what he was at and he seemed to forget nothing he had learned. Once he had mastered it, it was his.

Still, though I was at school and he busy helping his father, I managed to see a good deal of him. You see, I had to pass his house on my way up and down, and on the way home I used often—almost always, indeed—to call in at the workshop and sit in a corner on a heap of shavings while he worked, and we talked of the school and the other fellows and what I was learning.

And then there were many feast-days and holidays, and when he could he came down to join in our games ; or, what he liked better still, led us all up into the hills for a whole day's rambling.

He was the leader of us all, and when he was

there everyone gave him that place without question.

Not that he claimed it. It was just that we all felt, as the others had felt before I came, that he *was* the leader because he was the strongest and deftest and cleverest of us all. He could throw and catch a ball better than anyone I ever saw. His hands were wonderful, his long slim fingers were alive to their tips and very strong. And as for running, no one could come near him.

And then he was so altogether fair and right-minded. I have often seen the others come up to the workshop about something that was in dispute among them. And he would listen quietly to all they had to say, going on with his work all the time. Then he would perhaps put a question or two and look them through and through with those great clear eyes of his, and then he would say at once what he thought was right, and would go over the matter again with them and show them why it was right. And we none of us ever disputed his decisions.

When he was in our games, too, there was never any quarrelling, as there nearly always was when he was not there. For he saw to it that we played straight and would stand no nonsense about it. So that the games we had when he was there were the best we ever had.

With the very little ones, too, those who were not big enough to join in our rough sports, he was kindness itself.

Often, after getting us properly started, he

would go off to the youngsters and set them playing their own favourite games—marriages and funerals, caravans and robbers, sheep and wolves—and if they wanted to dance he could get more tunes, and livelier ones, out of the reed-pipe than anyone else in the village.

And then, to give them a rest, he would tell them a story, and in the pauses of our own games we would see them all clustered round him like bees on the comb, with eager faces and dancing eyes, or maybe rolling with laughter. For he looked at things in new ways and had very humorous ways of putting them, and it was that that made his stories so unforgettable. Often and often I wished myself sitting there among them, listening to him instead of being bumped about and worried by Nachor and the other big fellows, for, you see, I had not had much chance of playing games at Ptolemais and they were all new to me.

I remember coming up one day with a big bruise on my forehead. He was busy finishing off a yoke with a little two-handed-plane, and he kept going over and over it, though it seemed to me polished as smooth as a piece of ivory, and I said as much.

"Ah—don't I wish I could make all my yokes of ivory, Little Azor! They would be so smooth and cool to the neck. But they might be heavy, and as I can't make them of ivory I must get this oak as like it as I can. You see, I always think of the patient beast that will wear it, and I want him

to say, ' Thank you, brother, for making my yoke
so easy '. . . . A happy yoke makes the burden
light. You can't possibly be too careful over
your yokes. And it's the same with plow-
handles. They ought to be as smooth as ivory or
they gall the hand. . . . What have you done
to your forehead now ? "

" I . . . I fell."

" Yes ? . . . You are generally steady on your
feet, Little Azor. What was it made you fall ?
. . . or who ? "

" It is nothing, Jesus," said I, in some confusion,
for I saw he suspected what had happened. " It
will soon be all right again."

" Was it Nachor again ? " he asked, with his
eyes on my face, and seeing, I knew, right into
me.

But I would not tell him, and he smiled and
said, " Nachor is needing another thrashing, I
think, for the good of his soul. He is a wild bull
of Bashan and puts his strength to ill-use at
times. He needs reminding."

But all this was the boyish side of him, which,
of course, appealed to me most at that time.
There was another side which I recall now with
feelings deeper than I can put into words.

Often I have sat in my corner of the workshop
of an evening, when some of the neighbours
would gather there to discuss things with Joseph,
while he and Jesus were busy finishing some work
that was urgently needed. For Joseph was
among them what Jesus was among us boys and

girls, a clear-headed thinker and an absolutely just and fair-minded man. So most of their disputes—and they were many—came up to the workshop for settlement, and few ever dreamt of going against his judgment.

And all the news brought into the village by travellers or traders came up there for discussion also, and at times the discussion waxed hot. For the hand of Rome was heavy on us, and the taxes were unbearable, and the tax-gatherers unscrupulous and hated by all.

How we all—down to the very smallest—longed for the deliverance that had been so long promised and so much longer delayed !

They were doubtless very narrow and very ignorant, those old villagers. And when they would grow hot and excited over their hopes of another rising of the people that should drive the Romans into the sea, even I, small as I was, knew how foolish all such talk was. For I had lived at Ptolemais, and had seen the Roman legionaries and the wonder of their organisation and discipline, and I knew that if it came to fighting it would be our people who would be driven into the sea, not the Romans.

And the land was still full of the crosses on which hung all that was left of the rising under Judas of Gamala, though they were mostly in Judea, and I only saw them later when we used to go up to the Passover. But our people were slow to learn.

As they talked and wrangled and cursed and

boasted, the boy would go quietly on with his work, listening to it all, and now and again looking at this one and that with those wonderful seeing eyes of his, which seemed to pierce right through the fog of their talk to the minds and hearts that lay behind it. But he never said anything—until they had gone, and then he and his father would quietly discuss them, and their concerns, and their ideas—kindly, but, as I now recognise, very shrewdly and wisely. And that side of the boy impressed me deeply.

At times he seemed to me many, very many, years older than he actually was—so full of thought, so absorbed in things that were beyond me, and at such times his eyes would look larger and deeper than ever.

Often, at dusk, if they were not over-pressed with work, he would go off up the hill, and the first time I saw him going so, alone, I ran out after him to join him in his walk.

But he put his two hands gently on my shoulders and said very quietly, " Not to-night, Little Azor, —to-night I must go alone. I want to think," and he bent and kissed me and went on up the darkening hillside.

And as I went slowly back into the house the deep tender look in his eyes was with me, but it was the deepness of them that struck me most. When that look was in his eyes he seemed to me a man and very far above me, and I was afraid he would never be a boy again.

But the next time I saw him he would be just

as I liked him best, like an elder brother to me, but a very kind and clever one.

Always on the Sabbath, when we went down to the synagogue, he let me sit beside him among the other men, and very often I would push my hand into his as we sat, for the joyful feeling of brotherliness and comfort it gave me. For there was very much more in the feel of his hand than in any other person's I ever met. And I could always tell by the movement in his hand if he liked what was said or not.

CHAPTER IV

OF THE COMING OF TOBIAS

I WAS loitering about in the village on my way home from school one day when the boy hailed me and we went on together. He had been delivering some work at one of the far houses.

As we passed the little oak-grove where Naggai, the shepherd, lived when he was at home—he was the father of Nachor, the bull of Bashan, who had bruised my forehead that other day—we heard a strange little short-cut cry of something in pain.

Jesus leaped over the stone wall and I scrambled after him. And there we found Naggai and Nachor, and they were busy hanging a little dog from the branch of a tree. Nachor was laughing and pulling down its legs to end it.

Jesus sprang at him and hurled him on to his back. Then he lifted the wriggling little thing in his arms to ease its choking, and began loosening the cord round its throat.

" Why—Naggai ? Why do you hang him ? " he cried hotly.

" Well—it's like this," said Naggai, scratching his head, and looking at us very much as one of his own sheep would have done. " He wakes the baby with his barking, and the wife said we must be rid of him. And yesterday he killed one of the neighbour's hens. And he looks at the sheep at times as if he'd like to chase them, and once a dog begins chasing the sheep, you know. . . . And so I thought I'd best make an end of him."

" Will you give him to me ? "

" You can have him and welcome, if you'll be answerable for him."

" What's his name ? "

" Well . . . we call him Sheitan, for he's always in mischief."

" That is no name for a dog. I will give him a new and better name."

" And welcome. He's yours, but you'll have to be answerable for him."

" I'll answer for him," said Jesus, and we climbed back over the wall, he carrying the little dog in his arms.

He was a rather ugly little dog, with wiry dark-brown hair and quick brown eyes and a bushy tail; but now his eyes were dazed and unhappy, and he lay quietly in the boy's arms, looking sleepily up into his face and seeing nothing else, and now and again trying feebly to wag his tail.

" What will you call it ? " I asked, as we climbed the hill.

" I shall call him Tobias," he said, smiling, " after the dog in the old story. They don't tell us the dog's name in the story. But he belonged to Tobias and followed him everywhere and was his friend, as my little Tobias will be to me." And as we went he told me the story of Tobit and Tobias and Sara and Edna.

"I have always loved that little dog," he said. "I have always thought of him as a very plain little brown dog, but he was very faithful, and I shall love to have one of my own."

When we reached the workshop Joseph was hard at work there, and Mary was on her knees among the shavings searching for something she had lost.

"What have you got there, little son?" she asked, sitting up on her feet and gazing at him.

"A little dog, Mother," and he put the ugly little dog down among the shavings, where it stood shakily and looked up at him.

"A little . . . dog!" said Mary, staring at it in surprise, and Joseph stopped for a moment to look on.

"It is very ugly," said Mary. "Whose is it?"

"He is mine," said Jesus. "You see, Mother, Naggai was hanging him, and we came along just in time to save him, and so he gave him to me."

"But . . ." said his mother. "We don't need a dog. What do you want with it?"

"I saved his life and he loves me. I want him for a friend." At which his father laughed rather discouragingly.

"You have such strange ideas at times, my son," said his mother, looking at him with that wonder in her eyes which I had often seen there but did not understand.

And as to the ugly little brown dog, I was not surprised. For, you see, dogs were not held in any esteem among us. Indeed the very word was used as a term of scorn and reproach, and the idea of having a dog for a friend was very surprising.

Mary said again, " It is a very ugly little dog."

And Jesus answered her softly. " He has beautiful eyes and beautiful little white teeth. And he loves me because I saved his life. And I love him because I saved his life. When you save anyone's life you can't help loving him. But what are you searching for, Mother ? "

" I have dropped a farthing somewhere here and I cannot find it. See now, little son, find me my farthing and you shall keep your ugly little dog."

" We will find it," and we set to work, he sweeping up all the shavings with the little broom of twigs with which he always swept the floor, and I groping round after him. And at last we found the farthing hiding under the box of nails.

He carried it in triumph to his mother and then knocked together a little box and half-filled it with sweet-smelling cedar shavings, and put it in a corner and Tobias inside it.

" That is where you will live, little Tobias," he said, and Tobias licked his hand and turned himself round three times in the box and settled himself happily to sleep.

And after that, wherever Jesus went little Tobias was at his heels and they were very great friends.

When he was working, Tobias would sit on the bench watching his every movement. If a little dog could have done carpentering I am sure Tobias might have become a first-rate carpenter. And he looked so wise and understanding that Jesus talked much with him.

If only Tobias had been able to tell us what they talked about when they two were alone together he would have had many interesting things to tell. For when Jesus went up the hill by himself, and would not let even me go with him, little Tobias went always at his heels.

CHAPTER V

OF THE HILLS, THE POOL AND THE GREAT ROAD

I REMEMBER the whole holiday when the boy took a company of us up into the hills as he had promised.

The others had heard of our swimming in the pond and were all eager to do the same. But as it was a long tramp, and none of them had ever swum in their lives, their parents had forbidden them to go near the place unless Jesus was with them. Him they could trust to look after them.

There were about a dozen of us, besides Jesus and Tobias. Nachor, the son of Naggai, was there, and little Tobias looked at him askance and kept out of his way, as though he remembered that Nachor had tried to hang him. And there were Neri, the son of Jotham, the smith, but he was a very small boy, not big and burly like his father— and Arni, whose mother was a widow, and Jessai and Eber, the sons of Mattathias, the corn-merchant. These I remember specially because they came near to being drowned.

We all took our food with us in linen bags over our shoulders, and we felt like an army as we travelled up the hills and into the valleys until we came in sight of the pond.

It was a good year and the vines and figs and olives were laden with young fruit, and the ground was thick with flowers of every colour you could think of, except black. And the sky was blue without a cloud, and the hills were beautiful right up to their tops where the rocks showed through.

At sight of the pond we all started running, though we had, some of us, felt tired a moment before.

Jesus and Tobias got there far ahead of the rest. He pulled off his tunic as he ran, and jumped into the water and was swimming about, with Tobias trying his best to keep up with him, by the time we got there.

The others were all for rushing in to do the same, and I cried to Jesus to stop them, for I remembered how long it took me to learn and I was not sure that it would come as natural to them as it had done to him.

I had never told him about my own experience, for in the light of his it would have made me look awanting, and I desired to stand well with him.

He probably thought they could all do just as he had done, and did not understand my fears. Anyway, nothing would stop them, my small voice least of all, and they all rushed in laughing and shouting.

Nachor, in his usual headlong way, plunged towards the middle where Jesus and Tobias were, and Neri and Arni and Jessai and Eber all went after him. But as soon as they no longer felt the ground under their feet they lost their heads and thrashed wildly with their arms, and floundered about and began to sink. And then they screamed and it was all we could do to get them out again.

Jesus got hold of Nachor by the hair after he had gone down bellowing like one of Bashan's bulls, and dragged him along till his feet touched ground again. And I remembered afterwards how little Tobias barked and barked all the time as though exulting over Nachor and wishing he had been left to drown.

Then Jesus went back for Arni, who was screaming loudly but keeping his head above water somehow, though his eyes were starting out of his head with fear.

I managed to haul in little Neri, who was not far out, and then Jesus and I pushed out together for Jessai and Eber who had been the last to go in and had both sunk once and come up gasping and choking. However we got them in safely ; and we two, and the five who had thought swimming such an easy matter but had found that it was not, lay in the sun on the bank till we felt all right again.

And presently Jesus said to me, " Why could they not swim when I could ? "

" I think it was because they grew frightened when they could not feel the ground."

He nodded—" I never thought about it. It seemed to me as easy as running. And I supposed it would be the same with them."

" You do not know fear," I said.

And after thinking that over he said, " I do not think I do. . . . Though I was afraid when I saw Nachor go under."

" That was different. You were afraid for him, not for yourself."

" I am going in off the tree," he said, jumping up and running round the pond, and I followed him.

There was no need to tell the others not to go in again. They had had a fright and were content to sit and watch us. But presently we swam in to the wide-staring eyes on the bank and offered to show them in the shallow water how one had to learn to swim.

But none of those who had ventured before would try again, and the others were very timid, and I was sure none of them would ever become swimmers.

So we ate a meal there, and then went on over the hills to the Great Road that runs from the sea to Damascus and the Desert. And we lay there all afternoon among the rocks of the hillside, watching all that passed.

That was a thing we always enjoyed. For the traffic of that road, as on the other road, south of our village, was unceasing, and full of excitements.

There were endless lines of camels swaying slowly along, and as the wind blew towards us we could smell the odours of the rich spices they carried.

And we guessed as to what was in some of their

great top-heavy packs which always looked as if
they might topple over and carry the camel with
them.

And there were herds of oxen, lowing pitifully,
and flocks of bleating sheep ; and the wild-look-
ing men in charge of them were savage and cruel
and beat them unmercifully. For they were all
frightened and upset at being so far from the
places they knew, and at the strange things they
encountered on the road.

Once we saw a herd of cattle break away and
try to get off the road. And it was because some
carts passed them carrying great heavy cases—
things you did not see very often, and never I
suppose on the South Road.

But I had seen such at Ptolemais and knew what
they were.

At sight and smell of the cattle in the road a
dreadful roaring came from the big cases, and
Jesus said in surprise, " There are wild beasts in
them."

And I said, " Yes, they are going to Rome for
the games,—lions and tigers and other things,
and they are always hungry."

" It is hard for them," he said gently, and
stroked little Tobias who was whimpering by
his side.

Then in clouds of dust, there came troops
and troops of Roman soldiers, very hot and
tired, but still marching with steady, heavy tread,
with the sunshine flashing on their breastplates
and the short swords at their sides, and twinkling

on the long spears they carried over their shoulders.

And at sight of them some of the boys murmured curses, and said under their breath the things they would like to do to them.

But Jesus said nothing—only watched them gravely and his face was very sad.

And that day, as it happened, there passed by some very great man with chariots and horses and a mighty company—soldiers and slaves, white men and black men and yellow men, and banners and trumpets and two great gray beasts which lumbered along uncouthly, the like of which some of the others had never seen before in their lives.

But I knew them for elephants, for I had seen such stacking logs at Ptolemais.

" It will be King Herod himself," said Nachor, and it may have been, for no king could have made a greater show, unless it was Caesar himself from Rome.

And the others talked and talked, and there was no end to their chatter, for some of them had never seen the like and they talked much foolishness.

But Jesus was quite silent, only he lay watching it all with his chin in his hands and his eyes missing nothing. And only when the soldiers who marched in front scattered the wayfarers, and drove them headlong off the road to make way for the chariots, did his lips pinch tightly and there was a frown on his face, and I heard his feet behind kicking the ground.

" It's time the Deliverer came to rid us of all
that," said Nachor gloomily.

" The Teacher says he is coming," squeaked
little Arni.

" Ay ?—and when ? " asked Nachor, with
scorn in his voice.

" Very soon now, he says."

" The sooner the better. We've waited long
enough," growled Nachor. " When he comes
we'll fling all those Romans into the sea and make
an end of them, and then we shall rule all the
world instead of them. I hate all Romans, with
their taxes and their laws."

" The sun is setting," said Jesus, jumping up,
" and we've a long way to go. Give me your hand,
little Arni," and we all trailed after him.

The moon was like a silver shield hung on the
dark sky before we reached our own hills, and the
night was very beautiful. The plain as we
crossed it looked very wide and lonely, and the
white cap of Hermon peeped at us over the lower
heights of Lebanon. We seemed to be the only
living things abroad that night in all that land,
and the smaller boys were timid at the largeness
and emptiness of it.

So Jesus, as he often did, told us stories as we
went. And that night, perhaps because of what
we had been seeing, they were all about the great
deeds that had taken place round about us. He
told us of Deborah and Barak, and King Josiah,
and Gideon, and Saul and Jonathan and David.
And the little ones had no time to be afraid of

the shadows and the things that might be roaming about the great plain.

For when Jesus took to telling stories you forgot everything else and did not want to lose one word. For he told things as though he had really seen them himself, and he made you see them too.

CHAPTER VI

Of the Right Making of Yokes

TIME runs quickly when one is young. But the passing months and years only brought Jesus ben Joseph and myself into closer friendship.

As next-door neighbours, and somewhat apart from the other houses of the village, it was natural that most of our spare time should be spent together.

He was, as a rule, kept very busy in the workshop, for his liking for making yokes, and the care he put into the perfect finish of them, was beginning to make them much sought after. People came from very long distances to get them, and would wait till his were ready sooner than take anyone else's.

" You see," I heard a man say to him, one day when I was sitting in a corner of the workshop trying to draw Tobias into a game, " the beasts never complain when they're wearing one of your yokes. They're so well-shaped, and so smooth and easy to the neck, that they never get irked, and they do twice as much work."

" I am glad," said Jesus, and I can see again the quick, bright look on his face as he looked up at him from his work for a moment.

" And I'll tell you another thing too," said the
man. " It's my belief they tell one another
about them. Yes, I know it sounds queer "—
and he gave a little laugh as though in excuse of
his foolishness—" but after I'd got that first yoke
the other beasts wouldn't be easy with their old
one, and I could hardly get them to pull, no matter
what I did. So I had to fit them all out with
them and this one will make the last pair happy."

" I'm glad they like them," said Jesus, running
his hands questioningly along the yoke to make
sure it was quite all right, " and that they tell one
another. It would be hard to think they couldn't
speak to one another. They are not deaf and
they are not dumb."

" That's so, but it's queer to think of beasts
talking to one another."

" Balaam's ass talked even to his master ! "

" Ah ! . . . He was a queer one, he was. . . .
I met another the other day, and he was asking
after you——"

" An ass ?—asking after me ? "

" It wasn't an ass. It was a boy. But he was
a queer one. It was down Sharon way. I'd been
with a load to Joppa, and it was among the hills
as I was coming back. I was giving the beasts a
rest and he came striding along and he sat down
beside me and we talked. . . . My ! but he was
a queer one ! "

" Why was he a queer one ? And who was he ?
Did you get his name ? "

" Of course, and gave him mine. He said he

was John ben Zechariah, and his home was at Hebron."

"He's my cousin," said Jesus eagerly, stopping his work to follow this up. "Tell me about him. It's years since I've seen him. What's he like?"

"Well, he's a well-grown lad, taller than you and maybe stronger, though you look fairly fit yourself. But you're better to look at than him. His hair's like a horse's mane, all down his back— never been cut since he was born, I should say."

"Of course. He's a Nazarite."

"He's a wild one to look at anyway—all hair— coat and all, and a big leather strap round him to keep him all together. And he told me he sleeps out all weathers and roves all over the country. I expect he'll be coming up here to see you one day."

"I wish he would. I'd love to see him again. I have searched for him at each Passover but never found him. If you meet him again will you tell him how glad we'd be to see him?"

"I'll tell him, but I'm not very like to meet him. He roams the hills and goes where he will. I have my work to do and my beasts to see to."

"How came he to ask after me?"

"It was this way—I'd eased off the yoke of my two beasts that had the bad one, because they were fretting at it, and we got talking of yokes, and I showed him yours and told him how the beasts liked them, and he asked where they were to be had so that he might tell others about

them. And when I told him it was Jesus ben
Joseph up at Nazaret that I got them from, he
said, like you did—' Why, he's my cousin. Some
day maybe I'll go up there and see him.' That's
how it was. And now I must get along. I'm
right glad all my beasts will be happy now."
And he paid for the yoke and was going, when he
turned and said, " I was forgetting, I want a
goad too."

" I don't make goads and never will," said
Jesus. And the man stared at him.

" Why then ? You can't drive oxen without
the goad."

" Treat them properly and they'll need no
goads."

The man looked at him, and then wagged his
head and said, " Your life hasn't lain among beasts,
my lad—mine has," and he went on his way.

I got on well at school and was good friends
with most of the others—except Nachor ben
Naggai whom I never liked. He was rough and
irksome to us smaller ones, and whenever I looked
at him I always saw him and his father hanging
little Tobias.

But at lessons I got on well because I had a
good memory, and my mother had taught me
much of the Book of Praise of which she was very
fond. Of the Law and the other teachings I
learned a good deal and could repeat long passages
without a mistake. But it was all just memory
and there was much that I did not understand the
meaning of.

And often, when Jesus and Tobias were going up the hill of an evening, if he wanted me with him he would give a shout outside, and I would run out and join him with another shout that told him how glad I was, and we would all go on together.

And then he would ask me what I had learned at school that day, and would explain it all to me and make it all clear in a most wonderful way.

For he thought long and deeply over things while he was working, and he asked his father and discussed them with him, and he was never satisfied until he understood a thing properly. And he listened to and pondered over all that the neighbours talked about when they came and sat in the workshop of an evening. And so he knew pretty nearly all that went on in the village, and indeed, outside it too.

On one such walk I remember him telling me of a great piece of luck a man in the village had just had.

It was Amos ben Rhesa, who had a piece of ground just outside and made a scanty living by tilling it.

He had taken a sudden fancy to a neighbour's plot and nothing would satisfy him till he got it, though it was no better ground than his own.

However, he had a fancy for it, and to buy it he had to sell his own piece and pretty nearly everything he had—his wife's little ornaments and even some of her clothes. And the neighbours said he was mad.

But a month after he had bought the ground and was hard at work tilling it, he came on a box buried in the earth and it was full of treasure—gold and some jewels, and now he was a rich man and talked boastfully of going away with his wife and two sons to live in Kaphar-Nahum. "And the neighbours are saying now," said Jesus, "that he must have lighted on it one day when he was rambling about there and knew all about it when he bought the land, and so he ought rightly to give a part of it to old Matthat ben Reu, from whom he bought it. But Amos won't have it so, and of course the land was his when he paid for it. Some men will do anything for money. I hope you'll never be like that, Little Azor."

"I won't," I said stoutly. "I don't care for money." And I had conscientiously to add, "but then I've never had any of my own."

At which Jesus laughed and said :

"You've never been tempted so you can be warned," and then, more gravely, "The hunger for it is an evil thing, and most men seem to have that hunger. We are all poor, and every poor man wants to become rich—well, nearly every one. There are some who are satisfied if they can pay their way without running into debt, as my father is. And truly, from all one sees and hears, I believe they are happier than the others. . . . What is going on down there ? "

We were up on one of the heights, and down below on the plain was Naggai's flock of sheep, the mothers loosely bunched together, the lambs straggling about, and all bleating and baaing disconsolately But there was no sign of Naggai, and they were some distance from their fold, which lay near the village, round the other side of the hill.

" Where can he be ? " said Jesus. " He shouldn't leave them like that. They'll scatter."

And then his keen eyes detected a small dark figure at the foot of the hills on the far side of the plain.

" He's lost some of them. Let's go down and help with these," and we raced down the hillside. " We'll fold them for him."

But that was easier said than done. The sheep did not know us or our voices, and refused either to be led or driven. In fact the more we tried the more unhappy they became, and we were like to do more harm than good, though Tobias kept well at our heels as· if to make sure that none of the blame should rest on him. So, as Naggai was still searching along the hillside, we set off to see if we could help him.

As we drew near we saw that he had with him one old ewe in great distress of mind, running aimlessly to and fro and calling incessantly in a pitiful voice, and one small lamb trailing wearily after her wherever she went.

" Hello, Naggai ? What's wrong ? " asked Jesus. And Tobias kept well away behind him and peered suspiciously at Naggai between his legs.

" This one should have two and she's only got

one. I don't know where the little devil's got to. And why couldn't she speak before we'd got nearly home ? Silliest beasts Jah ever made, are sheep," growled Naggai.

"We'll help you find it. Where have you been all day ? "

"All along the hill here, both ways."

So we spread out and searched all along the base of the hills, Naggai and the mother-sheep and lamb going one way, and Jesus and I and Tobias the other.

It was growing dark and we could not see far and could only poke about among the bushes and in the holes in the mounds.

"It's gone," I said, unhopefully, at last, as I grew weary of the search. " Perhaps some beast has had it."

"We must find it," said Jesus. "You'd not be able to sleep a wink, Little Azor, for thinking of it out here all alone in the cold and dark."

And at last we heard Tobias yelping excitedly some distance away, and running to him we found him dancing about in front of a deep hole, and in the hole was a very frightened little lamb just wakened up from his sleep.

So Jesus picked it up and put it over his neck, holding its front and hind feet in his hands. We shouted to Naggai and he came running up, with the other lamb round his neck, and the mother trotting beside him. Jesus held down his lamb for her to snuffle and we all set off across the plain.

" And it was Tobias found him for you, Naggai," laughed Jesus. " And you wanted to hang him."

" Ay, well! One never knows. But the wife's happier without him anyway."

He called to the other sheep as we came up to them and then strode ahead and they all trailed after him.

At the fold he let down the door and called them by name, and they ran in under his rod and settled down for the night, and we went up home through the village.

CHAPTER VII

Of his Ways with "The Family"

Jesus ben Joseph had a very curious power over all beasts and birds. But I think it was just that he loved them all so much that in some strange way they knew it and loved him in return.

When I once said something like that to him, I remember he said, "Yes, of course, I love them all. They are all of the family. I love them and so they love me. That's how it is in the world. For the most part you get what you give, Little Azor. Give people love and they will love you. Give them scorn and hate and you get that back. . . . But," he said, after thinking it over, " it's not always so. There are some one meets who seem to have no love in them, except for themselves. So they can't give any, and they are difficult to get on with. Nachor is like that now. He doesn't seem to care for anyone except himself, and it is not easy to love him."

" I hate him," I said, and I had good reason to, " and so do all the others."

" That does no good either to him or you."

" But if you try to be nice to him he only thinks you're a fool and he's twice as nasty to you."

" Have you ever tried to be nice to him ? "

" N—n—no ! I don't know that I have, because I know it would be no use. He'd only hit me in the face or screw my arm round."

" I know. He's very difficult. But there is some good spot in everyone if one can only find it."

" There aren't any in Nachor—at least none of us has ever found any."

One of his most usual and characteristic sayings was " I love." Where I or another boy would say " I like," with him it was always " I love." And that was just him all over. His liking for things and people was so great that it really was love. He did nothing by halves.

He loved to sit in the dusk of evening up on the hillside and watch the birds and little beasts busy about their little businesses.

I have sat with him there and seen the rabbits and coneys come out of their holes and hop all about him without the slightest fear, and they are surely the timidest beasts you can find.

And birds—I remember once as we were passing through a grove there was a sudden flutter of wings alongside us, and he stopped and stood looking up with his finger on his lips.

And just up above us was a nest, and the mother-bird was getting the little ones to fly. Three she got to the edge all right and pushed over, and they spread their baby wings and reached the ground all right, and went hopping and fluttering among the bushes.

But there was evidently another one that was too timid or too lazy to want to fly.

She scolded it and then, at last, she got down inside the nest, and ruffled herself up under the birdling till it had to get out, and it fell with a thud on the ground at our feet.

Jesus picked it up and soothed it, for it was going in and out like a little bellows.

The mother flew at him and round and round him, and at last lit on his hand and pecked angrily at it.

And he smiled and said, " Good little mother ! But I'm not going to hurt it, dear. . . . It's too frightened and bumped to try to fly again just now, and if we put it back into the nest you'll only try again to make it fly. . . . We'll take it home and give it a night's rest and to-morrow it will fly all right."

So he put it inside his tunic above the girdle and we set off home. And for a time the mother accompanied us, flying round and round him with little cries. And then she seemed suddenly to think it would be all right, and she left us and went back to the others.

And it was the same with nearly all birds and beasts. He seemed in some curious way to feel them kin to him, and they felt it and had no fear of him.

With the wilder beasts and birds it was different of course—hawks and eagles, and wolves and hyænas, but we were not very much troubled with them.

But I remember how we stumbled one day on

a fox's hole out on the plain, and there were some very small cubs playing about in the opening. And he picked one up and was stroking it when the mother-fox came trotting back, and Tobias and I got well away from her, for she looked ugly and we thought she would fly at us.

She seemed to count her cubs, and gave each one a hasty lick, and when she saw the one in Jesus's arms she stood and snarled up at him, and watched him anxiously as he stroked it. So he put it down and it ran to her, and she smelled it to make sure it was all right, and sent them all into the hole, and looked up again at Jesus and went in after them.

I asked him once what he felt towards those wilder things, and he said, " I would like to feel the same towards them, Little Azor, but they wouldn't let me if I tried. They but follow their nature in preying on their fellows, and so, I suppose, it's all right in some way, but . . . no, I don't understand it. . . . Perhaps some day it will be different," he said wistfully.

And presently he said, as if he was just thinking out loud :

" The wolf shall couch with the lamb,
   The leopard's lair shall be with the kids,
   The lion shall eat straw like an ox,
   The wolf and lion shall graze side by side, herded by
      a little child,
   The cow and bear shall be friends and their young shall
      lie down together.
   None shall injure, none shall kill."

" When ? " I asked, urgently.

" When ? " he said, coming back to himself again—" When the Deliverer comes and his Kingdom is established in full. But who can say when that will be ? . . . You and I may not live to see it, Little Azor. But come it will, for God has said it through the prophet."

" Our Teacher says it will be very soon."

" I wish he may be right. With all my heart I wish it. . . . It is worse to see men preying on their fellows than to know that the wild beasts do so. And they do, Azor. Men can be very cruel, crueller far than lions or bears. And it is worse in them, for the beasts know no better. A cruel man is worse than all the beasts in the world. When that good time comes there will be no more cruelty, either among men or beasts."

Many things come back to me as I recall those rambles of ours. One was his very great love for all things that grew and had life in them.

In the Spring-time the plain was covered with flowers of all colours, so that it looked, from the hill-top, like a great wonderful rich robe, richer and more beautiful even than the garments of the great ones we at times saw pass along the road to the coast or to Jerusalem.

But he very rarely plucked flowers, except just now and again for his mother. And he said to me once, when I had gathered a great bunch and dropped some of them in the road—" Ah, never do that, Little Azor ! It hurts them."

" Hurts them ? " I echoed, in surprise, for I had never thought of them so.

" Surely," he said, carefully picking up those I had dropped. " They have life in them and so they must feel it when they are killed. But I think they must feel it still more when they are thrown aside as worthless."

" But I've seen you pick them," I urged.

" My mother loves them as I do and feels about them as I do. But she is kept so busy in the house that she cannot see them outside as much as she would like, and so she asks me at times to bring her some. And her wishes are more to me than the feelings of the flowers."

" But," I said again, after thinking that all over, " we have to prune the vines and the fig-trees."

" That's different. It's to make them bear better, and perhaps they know it. If you had a finger or a toe that had gone rotten, and the physician told you that unless it was cut off you would lose your hand or your foot, or perhaps your life, you would bid him cut it off, no matter how it hurt. . . ." And then he said thoughtfully, in that way he had at times of thinking out loud, " And perhaps it's the same among men. . . . If a bad man is corrupting his fellows, and he can't be cured of his badness, it is better he should be cut off. . . . And . . . a good man . . . if by giving up his life he could save his village or his country, it would be a great thing for him to die. . . . There have been such and their deaths were glorious."

CHAPTER VIII

Of our Meeting with Cousin John

Little Arni, the one whom Jesus saved from drowning that day at the hill-pond, had gone with his mother to live in Nain, where her brother had offered her a home. She was very poor and had had hard work to make a living in our small village.

Jesus was fond of the lad. As he once said about Tobias, "When you save anything's life you can't help loving it."

Certainly he had saved Nachor's life at the same time, and I have no doubt he would have loved Nachor too—as he would have loved the wild beasts if they would have let him—but Nachor was as hard and thick-skinned as one of the elephants that piled the logs at Ptolemais, and he wanted no one's love.

And so, at times, when we could get a whole day off, we would go along the valley towards the Plain of Esdraelon and strike up through the olive groves and over the hills to Nain, to see Arni and his mother.

It was a glorious tramp, for the Great Plain, with the Kishon wandering through it in wide curves on its way to the sea, was a wonder in itself, and Jesus made it still more wonderful by the stories he told of the great things that had happened there. While we lay on our faces on a hill-top and ate our meal, he told of King Joram and Ahaziah, and Jehu the furious driver, and of Elijah and Elisha, and of Judith and the Assyrian King.

And there, just in front of us, was Mount Gilboa, where Saul and Jonathan were killed. And on the other side was Tabor. It was a wonderful place.

We were lying there one such day when Jesus, who had been gazing very intently across the valley towards Gilboa, said, "Who is this, I wonder?" And I saw, a very long way off, a small black figure coming from the direction of Mount Gilboa. It crossed the stream and came steadily on as though making straight for us, though it could not possibly see us lying there among the rocks of the hill-top.

"Who can it be?" I whispered, but I got no answer.

Jesus only lay and watched, but I knew that he was very full of something, by his eager face and the absolute quietness in which he lay. He seemed to me like a tightly-strung bow.

And when the stranger below drew near to the olive groves that lay about the foot of our hill, he suddenly sprang up and gave a great "Hallo! Hallo!" and Tobias barked loudly.

The stranger stopped and stared at us under

his hand, and then came striding on through the grove and straight up towards us.

Jesus ran down to meet him, with Tobias racing and bounding beside him, and I lay still and watched, though I had guessed by this time who it must be.

I recalled what that ox-man had said when he bought the yoke and wanted to buy a goad also.

There was no mistaking who this strange-looking figure was, and I stared my hardest at him. We had queer people passing through the village at times, but I had never seen anyone quite as queer as this.

In the first place his skin was burned red-brown with the sun, almost black—what you could see of it, and that was only part of his face and his arms and legs. And all the rest of him was shaggy hair. The hair of his head was, as the ox-man had said, like a horse's mane that had never been trimmed, and it tumbled wildly about him. And his coat was hair of some kind and very shaggy, and round his middle he had a wide leather band. His hand was hard and bony but looked very strong, and in it he grasped a long thick stick which was taller than himself.

"You are my Cousin John," I heard Jesus say, and he threw his arm round his neck and kissed him on the cheek.

"And you are Jesus ben Joseph!"—and the other held him off at arm's length to get a better sight of him.

"I've been hoping you would come," said

Jesus. "It's a long time since we've seen one another," and they came up the hill together.

And as they came John was gazing at Jesus all the time in the most curious, searching way. It might be to see how he had altered since they met. But his eyes were as strange as all the rest of him.

He had very bushy brows and his eyes were set deep under them, and they burned in their hollows like live coals in the dark.

"This is Azor ben Azor, my dearest friend," said Jesus, as I stood up to meet them. "Little Azor, it is my Cousin John."

"I know," I said. "I remembered him."

"Why—where have we met?" asked John, abruptly, almost harshly, and turned his great smouldering eyes on me.

"We haven't. But," I said, tearing my eyes away from his with an effort, for they held me as by a spell, and looking up at Jesus, "I remember what the ox-man told us."

"Ah, yes—the ox-man. He told us he met you down by Sharon, and what you were like. Little Azor forgets nothing. The ox-man said you might come up this way, and I've been expecting you ever since. I'm very glad you've come, John. I want to hear all you've been doing—and thinking."

"The doing is soon told. The thinking would take long. . . ."

His voice was vibrant and sonorous, but rather harsh. I thought he probably talked much aloud

to himself in the deserts where he lived, and perhaps shouted and sang. There was none of the
roundness and sweetness, as of a flute, or at times
as of a silver trumpet, that was in Jesus's voice.
Him it was a joy to listen to, no matter how long
he spoke. But John's voice was so harsh and
rasping that it was hard to endure for any length
of time.

"And this ? " he said, looking down at Tobias,
who, after a sniff or two, did not seem to like him
much and had got round to the other side of
Jesus.

"That's my other little friend Tobias."

"Your—friend ? " with surprise and a touch of
scorn.

"Yes, he belonged to Naggai, the shepherd.
But Naggai called him Sheitan and was going to
hang him, and Azor and I came along just in
time to save his life and Naggai let me have him.
He's a faithful little friend and I love him."

But John was not much concerned about either
Tobias or me. So we sat there quietly while the
cousins talked. And their talk sounded strange
to me.

"And you spend all your time in the open,
Cousin John ? Or was the ox-man telling us
tales out of his head ? " asked Jesus.

"Where should one live better than under
God's sky ? " and he threw his arms up with a
strange wild gesture.

"I love the open too," said Jesus, " especially
the hill-tops——"

" Ay—the hill-tops ! One feels nearer to God on the hill-tops. . . . And at night ! . . . Ah —the nights !—'The firmament showeth His handiwork ! ' . . . I make my bed with Mazzaroth—with Arcturus and Orion and the Pleiades . . . great bed-fellows ! And at dawn ! . . . the morning stars sing together ! I would not live in a house—no, not in Herod's palace."

" Truly—not there would any of us live. But in the winter storms, John ? How do you suffer them ? "

" There are caves without number down yonder if one needs them—ay, enough to shelter all Israel."

" But how do you live ? What do you eat, if you're for ever wandering on the hill-tops and never go home ? "

" Eat ? I eat what God gives me to eat. He feeds the ravens and He feeds me. The earth is full of things to eat—wild carobs, and honey, and now and again a fig, some dates, some grapes."

" And your father and mother ? What do they——"

" They dedicated me Nazarite for life to the service of Jah," broke in John, as though, it seemed to me, to fend off further questions about them, and I wondered if, maybe, they would have had him live otherwise.

" But how do you serve Jah by roaming about the hills ? " persisted Jesus.

" I am learning. Sometime I shall know. And you—— ? "

All the while he spoke his burning eyes were fixed hungrily on his cousin's face.

They were about as unlike one another as they could possibly be. For Jesus was the comeliest boy I ever saw, and it was joy just to look upon his face, and to watch his feelings in it, and the star-shine in his clear, steady eyes.

But John was rough and wild and unkempt, and he was harsh and abrupt, and his eyes were deep smouldering fires.

" I ? " said Jesus. " I live with my father and mother, and help in my father's business."

" You make ox-yokes," with a touch of scorn again.

" And good ones too. I serve Jah by making the best yokes that can be made."

" And life is corrupt and the world is going down into darkness."

" Deliverance will come."

" Ay ?—how and when ? " with a hungry look at him.

" With the promised Messiah. . . . But when . . . we know not. They say very soon now."

" Who say ? "

" The Teachers."

" Ah !—the Teachers ! False shepherds, most of them. They are so blind and deaf with their own learning that they cannot see Jah. They will never deliver the people—nor themselves."

" No !—the Messiah ! "

" And he will come ! He will come ! . . . He may be among us now if he is to come soon, as your Teachers say. . . . If we only knew ! "

He gazed devouringly at his cousin's face, so full of quiet strength and the joy of living and all the grace and spirit of youth.

I can see them yet, those two, as they sat among the rocks that day. And as I recall them they stir me again as they did then ;—John, all abristle outside and all aboil inside with the turmoil of his thoughts, jerking out his words in harsh abrupt sentences which sometimes ended and as often broke off short to let some other thought shoot out ;—Jesus, quiet, but vividly alive, restrained, but, as I well knew, as brimful of energy as the other, and so much more desirable as a friend.

I did not feel as if I could ever like John much, and indeed he did not look or speak as if he desired anyone to like him.

But, though he seemed scornful of his cousin's simple workaday way of life, there must have been something in him that pleased him—if one could imagine anything giving John pleasure. The mere thought of pleasure of any kind assorted ill with him. For he hardly took his eyes off Jesus, and at times the smouldering glow in them seemed to burst into flame. And once I heard him murmur under his breath, as it were just his thought breathing out unconsciously, " I wonder ! . . . I wonder ! . . ."

And I wondered what he wondered.

" Do you see the evil of men up your way ? "

he broke out again. " All up and down the
land it is the same. Everywhere I go. . . . The
villages, the towns, the country-sides . . . craft
and guile and self-seeking . . . and the wickedness
of Rome, and she rules the world. . . . And our
own princes . . . and our priests—it is the Devil
they serve, not Jah. And still he comes not . . .
nor makes any sign. . . . How long, oh Lord,
how long ? " and he flung his arms up again in a
great beseeching gesture.

" He will come," said Jesus quietly. " In
God's good time, be sure he will come, John."

" I grow sick with the waiting. Every day
but makes his task the harder."

" With God no task is hard. He made the
world. He will save it. Else why did He make
it ? "

" Ay—why ? why ? I often wonder. For He
can find no joy in it."

" It's a very beautiful world," said Jesus softly,
and his eyes roved lovingly from Gilboa to the
great plain with its silver river, and on to Carmel.

" But for the men in it. . . . All spoiled by
His own creatures. . . . Why does He suffer
them ? . . . Break it all up ! . . . Drown it as
in the time of Noah, and begin afresh ! "

" That would be to confess failure," said Jesus
thoughtfully. " And He cannot fail."

" A terrible world . . . a terrible world," said
John, and fell silent with the thought of it.

" You will come home with me, Cousin John ? "
said Jesus presently, for the sun was sinking towards

the sea beyond Carmel. " My father and mother would wish to see you, and you don't come too often."

" I would see them too. Joseph and Mary are dear to my father and mother. But I will sleep without, with Orion."

" You shall sleep where you will if you won't take my bed."

" I have not slept on a bed since I have had any say in the matter."

Jesus was about sixteen years old at the time when he and John met, and John was a little older. He was taller than Jesus and very lean and hard. But they seemed to me as different in nearly all things as the day is from the night, and I could never have felt towards John as I did towards Jesus.

CHAPTER IX

OF HIS HEIGHTS AND DEPTHS AND BREADTHS

LIFE teaches us all that at times things go on smoothly and quietly for a long while and then there comes a break and many changes.

It was so in our village. In those first seven years nothing out of the common seemed to happen. A few old people died, babies were born. Some people left and new ones came. But such changes were few.

Then came the greater ones. Jesus was eighteen—a boy no longer, but a grown man, doing man's work, and known far and wide as not only a clever craftsman, but as an absolutely upright man, and possessed of better judgment and greater wisdom than most.

He had always had a very thoughtful side, though in the earlier days, when with the rest of us, he was just a boy like the others. But even at that time, as I have told before, he was looked up to by us all because of his clearer common-sense and his strong will for all that he believed to be right. So we had all trusted him and accepted him as our leader.

I had been specially favoured with his love and friendship, and I loved him in return as I had

never before loved anyone.   I loved my mother,
of course.   But that was different.   Jesus ben
Joseph was the first who woke in me all those
other feelings of absolute devotion which between
a young boy and an older one mean so much.   It
was what David and Jonathan had felt for one
another.   I can never be grateful enough.   Jesus
was my hero and I worshipped him.

I had more opportunities than any of knowing
and loving him, for when I had learned all our
old teacher could give me at the school, I stuck
to my old wish to be a carpenter as Jesus was, and
I was allowed to help him and his father in the
workshop, and no better apprenticeship could I
have possibly had.

They were both skilled workmen, and what is
more, they loved their work and put their hearts
into it.   Men knew that if Joseph ben Heli or
Jesus ben Joseph fitted a door to their house and
a lock to their door, both would do their proper
service till they fell to pieces with old age.   If
they made a chest, it was a thing to treasure and
hand down to their children.   Their yokes and
plows, as I have told, were sought from afar.

And, working in their company, I learned much.
Not only to do best work, but, from all I heard in
the workshop, to think upon things, and, to some
extent, to comprehend men and their natures.
For, more than ever, the other men of the
village came up there to consult Joseph and Jesus
about their affairs, for they were a quarrelsome
lot ;   and   at   times   about   the   larger   affairs

outside, for their grievances under Rome were many.

As he grew to be a man Jesus became ever more thoughtful, and that habit of his of going up to the hill-top to think things out for himself grew upon him.

At times he would have me go with him, and those were times to remember. So gay and joyous would be his talk and the stories he told. He had endless stories, quite simple, but they started one thinking, and more often than not drove home into one's mind something he desired to fix there, as deftly and truly as he drove his nails in the workshop.

But at times we got upon deeper subjects, for he was often sorely troubled by the things we heard and saw among the village-folk. And there were times—and they grew ever more frequent— when he wished to go up there alone, with none but little Tobias, who gave him his heart, as I did. Yes, I have often thought that, if Tobias had only been gifted with speech, like Balaam's ass, what things he could have told. But I know well that he would not. For he was a faithful little soul and Jesus loved him dearly.

Joseph, his father, was growing old, and was often unable for his work. He was of a good age when he married Mary, and all his life he had worked hard.

So the heavier part of the work began to fall upon Jesus, and by degrees, also the leading part in the discussions in the workshop.

For years he had listened and thought, had said little but thought the more. So that now his mind was matured beyond his years, and when he spoke men listened to him. His thinking was so clear and direct that it went right to the root of any matter, and his words were so simple and weighty and so exactly right that none failed to understand him.

As a rule he spoke very gently, but if occasion arose, as at times it did, his speech could be like a sharp chisel, piercing deep, and his thoughtful eyes flamed fires.

The grave concentrated gaze with which he listened to each one who spoke to him was very disconcerting to such as had anything to conceal, and many had.

To each man with whom he talked he gave his whole mind absolutely, and each felt that all his concern was for the matter in question. And those deep comprehending eyes of his penetrated all subterfuges and looked deep into men's hearts.

It seemed to me, quietly watching him and them, that he always did his very best to get clearly into his mind their own complete and true points of view—to see the matter as they saw it. And then, bringing it to the touch-stone of his own larger and clearer vision, he would point out in a few pithy words—and as often as not in a crisp and novel little story—the error in their reasoning or the mistake in their doing, and give them his own clear-cut view of the matter. And if their mistake was a wilful one, and they tried to mislead him, or conceal anything in order to bias his judgment—and that was very usual with them, for it is very human to tell but half the truth when one is in the wrong—then his eyes would flame, the stars in them would become like little flashes of lightning, and his words would make them shrivel.

I have seen men three times his age shrink abashed before his scorching words and eyes, knowing well that they were in the wrong and had attempted to deceive him.

And such happenings always troubled him. I remember him one day saying sadly to me, when the offender had slunk off down the road, abashed but, I fear, muttering curses, " Little Azor, where are we getting to when men can act like that ? " and he was clouded for the rest of the day and spent the whole night on the hill-top.

But with it all he grew to a deep understanding of men. And I think it was that very deep desire to understand, and share fully with them all their troubles and all their hopes, that drew men to him and led them to unburden themselves as to no one else.

Joseph ben Heli died after a very short illness, and was buried in a tomb at the foot of the hill near the village. He was mourned sincerely by all, for all men had looked up to him because of his wisdom and his kindliness, and for the good work he always did.

Jesus felt his loss more than any, for he had learned from him all that the Teacher could not teach him, and he had always held his father above all other men.

His grief was greater than he allowed to show. He missed him at every turn. But he bore himself calmly. " For," as he said to his mother and me in the workshop, " we shall see him again," and of that I knew he was quite assured. But he seemed to grow suddenly much older, as though to fill his father's place.

After that, the work grew heavier upon us two, and we had to toil early and late to cope with it. Before long we had to get in another to help us, and Jesus chose Neri, the son of Jotham the smith. He was small but strong and sturdy, and very willing because he liked wood better than iron to work on. And he was always smiling and cheerful.

We all worked very happily together, all putting in the very best that was in us, as indeed one could not help doing, when Jesus was overlooking us.

The happiest days I had ever known were spent in that workshop, with its one side open to the plain below and the dark hills of Lebanon, where sunshine and shadow chased one another in perpetual games of hide-and-seek, and away in the distance the cap of Hermon shining white above them.

Mary would often come in from the house with her stool and her work and sit and chat with us, and the birds flew in and out and perched where they would and chirped and twittered confidently to us. And when the sun was hot the whole place was sweet with the smell of rosemary from Mary's two big bushes, and with pine and cedar, as Tobias, all abristle with shavings, and his black nose covered with sawdust, played about the floor with his mouse, or jumped up on to the bench where Jesus was working and watched all that he did with sharp expectant eyes. For to Tobias the hoped-for moment was when the sun sank behind Carmel, and the tools were hung up in their places, and the floor was swept clean, and the evening meal was eaten, and a word or a whistle from his master called him to company him up the hill.

Tobias's mouse was one of the many humours of the workshop. He discovered it one day among the shavings and gave chase. The mouse, by a happy instinct, ran up the first thing that offered chance of escape, and that was Jesus's leg. It scrambled right up into the bosom of his tunic and lay there quivering. And Jesus laughed and took it into his hand and soothed it, and then showed it to the panting Tobias, and with uplifted finger admonished him, " Little Tobias, this is one of the family and is not to be harmed ! " And Tobias understood, and thereafter played much with the mouse but never hurt it. But Mary was always rather doubtful of it.

Tobias went up the hill with him much oftener than I did, many times oftener, but in that matter understanding was vouchsafed me. And such times as Jesus called me to go with him were times of deep delight.

As I have said, as time passed, he sometimes spent the whole night up there. Whether he slept under the stars, as John did—with Mazzaroth and Arcturus and Orion and the Pleiades— I do not know. But I do know that he never showed any sign of weariness next day. Indeed, he would go up at times looking spent, after a long hot day's work, or still more after some disputation with some troubled and none too straightforward neighbour, and he would be at work again by sunrise, all himself, and as cheerful and happy as was his wont.

CHAPTER X

Of my Quest after two Fair Maids

THEN came another change in our lives, a change that meant more to some of us than we then knew.

My mother received word that her brother Matthat ben Nathan had died, leaving two daughters with no one to look after them and almost nothing to live on.

After thinking it all over carefully she decided that they must come to live with us in Nazaret. My earnings, and what she had from my father, would suffice us. We could build another room on to the house, a small one in a corner of the roof, for me to sleep in, and the girls could have my room.

She knew very little of them, but thought one of them was about my age. They lived in Kedesh, in the north country, not far from the Waters of Merom. And, to my great delight, it was decided that I should go and bring them down to Nazaret.

The room was put in hand at once. We borrowed three asses from a neighbour in the village, Peleg, who kept the inn and did a trade in fish from the lake.

He picked out for me his three best, or so he said, but either the others must have been very slow beasts indeed or I lacked the knowledge of how to induce mine to their quickest.

It was a three days' journey, and I had had little experience of travelling, except on foot about our own hills, and the yearly Passover journey to Jerusalem when we all went in company. And so the neighbours gave me much good advice; so much, indeed, that if I had heeded all their warnings I should probably never have started at all. Peleg's, however, was useful as the result of his own experience.

" Keep away from the Great Road as much as you can," he said. " Take rather the village tracks even if it takes you longer." He was to receive so much a day for the asses, but it was good advice all the same.

" Last time I came up from the lake," he said, " a devil of a Roman on a horse upset one of my beasts into the ditch and scattered all my fish. I put a curse on him and pray Jah he may suffer. So keep you to the village tracks and clear of all Romans, especially if they're on horses."

" Was your beast in the middle of the road, Peleg ? " asked Jesus quietly.

" Well . . . it was, but not by my will. I had five to look after, you see, and it had strayed a bit."

" So you were to blame, you see, and your curse will not work." And to me, he said, " Keep a civil tongue and your own counsel, Little Azor, and the side of the road if you have to go on it."

He still called me Little Azor at times, though I was growing quickly and even looked like topping him in time. But he was of so shapely a build, and bore himself so well and uprightly, that he looked taller than he really was. And there was such strength of calm unruffled wisdom in his face that he looked older than his years.

When he went up the hill of a night, at times he went heavily and slowly enough. But when he came down again his step was that of a mountain deer, light and full of life and spring, and his face was always placidly strong again.

So, in the early dawn one morning, I set off with my three asses on that great adventure, bearing with me a tablet from my mother to the two girls, and food for several days so that I should not be a burden on anyone on the way. And Jesus came down to the foot of the hill with me, and gave me a farewell kiss and many heartening claps on the shoulder when we parted.

"Be very circumspect, Little Azor, and may Jah have you in His keeping and prosper your going and coming!" were his last words, as he turned to climb the hill to his daily work.

A wonderful journey that was. Our great plain was carpeted with flowers of every colour one could think of, and growing so thick and close that at times it was difficult to find the track.

I made first for Cana, whose white walls shone in the distance, and from there headed straight

for the white cap of Hermon, though it lay far
beyond the end of my journey.

It was all a great joy to me.   Never was so blue
a sky or so bright a sun.   Away on my right hand,
as I topped the hills, that other blue streak was
the Great Lake, with the white walls and towers
of its busy cities and the gray and brown hills on
its far side.   And away on the left I could still
see Carmel, standing, as I well knew, with its feet
in the still greater sea.

But never surely were there slower asses than
those three of Peleg's.   They set their own pace
and nothing I could do sufficed to quicken it.
Beating might, but I was unused to asses, and
their gentle meekness left me at their mercy, so
our progress was slow.   I could have walked
faster, but we could not ask the girls to walk all
the way back with their belongings.

As we jogged slowly through Cana a man
stopped me in a crowd and said solemnly, " So
you have found them at last ? "

And I stared back at him and said, " Found
what ? "

" Your father's asses.   Are you not that son of
Kish who has sought them all these years ? "

It was in me to make some smart reply that
would have turned the laugh against him.   But
I could think of nothing till I was a good mile
past the village, and then it came to me that I
might have said, " Sir, had I known you were
here I would have come at once to claim the
greatest of them."

But maybe it was just as well, and when I remembered the counsel Jesus had given me, I was sure it was.

I slept that night in a little village on the other side of the hill towards Beth-Meron, and the next night at Gischala. And on the third day, after climbing up and down another range of hills, I drew near to Kedesh.

I stopped at the first house in the village and asked where Zerah and Zoe, the daughters of Matthat ben Nathan, lived, and a house on the hillside was pointed out to me.

As I came near it I saw a girl sitting on a stool spinning coarse flax with distaff and spindle. She gazed at me with surprise as I came steadily on with my three leisurely asses, and when I got quite close she stood up, staring hard, but never stopped her spinning.

I had not had much to do with girls, and none of our Nazaret maids had ever quickened my heart by one beat. But I thought this girl the most beautiful one I had ever seen.

She was, I guessed, somewhere about my own age. Her face was very sweet and comely, and she had black hair and large dark eyes with a little cloud of sadness in them. And she was slim and shapely.

Yes, my heart beat quicker as I looked at her, and I felt suddenly tongue-tied and rough and uncouth before her, and very aware of the dust that was thick upon me.

My little ass stopped right in front of her, as we

two stared at one another, and with an effort I managed to say, " I am seeking my cousins, Zerah and Zoe, the daughters of Matthat ben Nathan."

And she cried, in a voice like a flute, " Zerah ! "

Then in the dark doorway behind her another girl appeared and stared at me also.

Now if the first girl had taken my breath with her beauty, how shall I try to tell of her sister Zerah ?

It is beyond me. Though I added word to word in a great procession I could never make you see Matthat's Zerah as she appeared to me that day. For she was beautiful beyond all words to tell.

She was several years older than her sister Zoe, and so in the full splendour of her maidenhood— tall, and of a very gracious dignity : dark like her sister and with the same sadness in her large dark eyes.

" He says he is our cousin and has come to seek us," said Zoe, and I was grateful to her, for I could only stare dumbly at the two of them. I had not known that such beauty existed, and it overpowered me and made me feel like a log of wood. But I was grateful that the log had eyes to see with.

Bits out of the Song of Songs bubbled and sang in my head and in my heart as I gazed mutely at those two girls.

" Who is this glowing like the dawn, fair as a mirror, clear as the sun, overawing like an army with banners ?

You stand there straight as a palm.
Your body is a bundle of wheat encircled by lilies.
Your waist is round as a goblet.
Ah, you are fair, you are fair,
With dove-like eyes.
The dark stream of your hair is as a flock of goats on
    the slopes of Gilead.
Your cheeks are like slices of pomegranate.
Your neck is like David's tower.
Your eyes are like the Pools at Heshbon.
A King's Daughter!"

And in that I was right, for their mother traced direct from Elmadam, the son of Er, who was of the line of David, the King.

The great dark eyes of the elder girl rested searchingly upon me, calmly questioning, seeming to look deep into my heart—just, I thought, as Jesus ben Joseph's eyes looked into people and seemed to read their innermost thoughts.

But I had nothing to hide from her, and least of all the wonder and joy the sight of her and her sister were to me.

So I gave her back look for look, and perhaps she read in my eyes or in my heart somewhat of all I was feeling.

" You are then the son of Miriam, our father's sister ? " she asked, and her voice was like her sister's, but even more round and mellow and flute-like.

" I am."

" And your name ? "

" I am Azor ben Azor."

She nodded. She had no doubt heard from

her father that his sister had married Azor ben Amon of Ptolemais.

" And wherefore do you seek us ? "

" My mother heard of your father's death— peace be with him !—and that you were left lonely. She would have you come and live with us at Nazaret. See—here is her own word ! " and I pulled out my tablet and handed it to her.

She read it at a glance, and said, " You will stop the night with us, Cousin Azor ? The beasts can go into the walled garden there. There is little they can destroy, but there are many thistles they can eat. I will get you water to wash with."

She and her sister went into the house, and I joyfully led my three meek little asses into the neglected garden, and when I came back there was a basin of water and a towel on the doorstep.

When I had washed I felt very much better, but I still lingered shyly outside. For my heart was leaping wildly and my head was in a con- fused whirl of happiness.

I felt like one to whom has come unexpected good fortune. And amid it all I was saying to myself again and again, " What will Jesus think of them ? "

And I knew that he would delight in them, for he loved all beautiful things.

Then, while I still hesitated at going into the house of such wonderful maids, Zerah came to the door again and looked out and cried, " Where —oh, you are there, Cousin. Why don't you come in ? The supper is ready," and I followed her in, all agog with expectation.

The house was of fair size but very sparely furnished, and the meal was of the simplest. But it was enough for me to feast my eyes on those two most beautiful maidens.

As we ate, Zerah quietly drew from me all she desired to know—about my mother and myself and Nazaret and our home. And Zoe listened with sparkling eyes, and looked up at me as I told, in a way that filled me with a great and novel joy. I had never had anyone regard me so admiringly before. It made me think of the way little Tobias sat watching Jesus as he worked. But it was much greater joy to be watched by Zoe than by Tobias.

I told them all about Jesus and Mary and Joseph and Tobias, and everything and everybody else I could think of, and I had never known such joy in talking before, nor that I could talk so well. But there was something about them that went to my head, and maybe to my heart, and I was no longer Little Azor but felt myself a very Big Azor, and very rich in having two such wonderful maids for cousins.

And they enjoyed listening, I could see. For it was the opening of a new life for them, and the birth of new hope where there had been only clouds and sadness before them.

When we had finished supper, Zerah said, " We are very grateful to your mother and you, Cousin Azor, and we will gladly come with you to

Nazaret," and perhaps my face showed how glad
I was.

" And when, Cousin Zerah ? "

" We would like one day to wind up our small
affairs here, and the next day we will go."

And then, very quietly and simply, she told me
of themselves. How their father had been a
merchant, trading with Damascus and Tyre and
Sidon, and how one of his principal debtors, a
Greek, had robbed him of almost all he had, and
the anxiety of it had stricken him down, and he
had died leaving them almost nothing. And
they had been very forlorn and hopeless, not
knowing what they could do, and had even of
late been selling their furniture and ornaments
in order to eat.

And so my coming, with that warm invitation
from my mother, had been like a Godsend to
them, and their hearts went out to us.

CHAPTER XI

Of our Treasure-Trove

On the next day but one we started on the journey to Nazaret. And if the journey up to Kedesh had been wonderful to me, how shall I tell of the wonder of the journey home?

Then, my only companions were the incorrigibly slow little asses, and the way had seemed long. Now I shared the road with the two most beautiful beings I had ever met, and the way seemed all too short. If it had been ten times as long it would not have been long enough for me.

The two girls rode the other asses, with some of their bundles tied on to them, and the rest I piled on to my beast and walked beside it. To that they raised objections at first, but I assured them that walking was more to my liking than riding, and that I could have come in half the time if I had not had the asses, only that we could not expect them to walk and carry their bundles as well.

They had spent most of their lives in Kedesh, so this journey by the country paths, up and down the hills and across the streams, was a new joy to them.

Zerah, by reason of her three or four more

years, and having been in charge of the household since her mother died, and sharing her father's troubles, was the graver of the two, as she was, I suppose, the more beautiful.

But Zoe, who looked up to me, grew and grew upon me till I thought there never could have been a sweeter maid in Israel.

We laughed and talked and enjoyed every minute of each day, and Zerah listened and joined in at times, but for the most part she was grave and thoughtful.

I told them much of my chief friend, Jesus. In fact I talked so much about him—which was only natural, seeing that he was the dearest and greatest thing in my life, along with my mother, only there was more to tell about Jesus—that I remember Zerah saying, with her grave sweet smile, " He must be a very wonderful man to fill your heart and mind so full of him."

" Oh, he is," I said. " He is the best and most wonderful one you can imagine. You'll love him, Zerah. And he will love you. He loves all beautiful things, and all flowers and birds and beasts, and they all know it and they all love him. You can't help loving him."

And Zerah smiled again that grave sweet smile which made her face so rarely beautiful. But Zoe's happier laugh and her young bright face, and the way she looked up to me, set my blood racing, and I was happier, I think, than ever in my life before.

They rejoiced in everything we saw—in distant

Carmel and a silvery gleam of the Great Sea, in the glimpses of the blue lake on the other side whenever we topped a hill—in Tabor and Gilboa, and especially in the wonder and beauty of our flower-decked plain.

" It is a fairer land than ours," said Zoe, joyously. " I am glad we have come. And perhaps there are no wolves here in the winter."

" I have never seen one yet. Naggai has to guard his sheep in the winter, but they have never come near us."

" We used to hear them nearly every night. And if the winter was a hard one they would come right into the village. I cannot see why wolves should be," said Zoe.

" I know. That is one of the hard things to understand. . . . Even Jesus cannot understand it, though he says there must be some reason for them since they are all of the family."

" The family ? " said Zerah.

" He says all things—all beasts and birds and flowers and trees are of God's family, as well as men and women. But even he cannot understand why bears and lions and wolves are in it."

" It is hard to understand," she said.

" But he says that men who prey on their fellows, and are cruel and brutal, are worse than bears and lions——"

" They are," and I thought she was thinking of her father and the Greek who had robbed them.

" But he says too that sometime it will all be made right, and the wolf and the cow will couch together, and the lion will eat straw like the ox——"

"That's out of the prophet," said Zoe.

"And does he say when it will be ? " asked Zerah.

"When the Deliverer comes and rules over all things."

"May it be soon ! " she said softly.

It was the afternoon of the third day when we came to the foot of our hills, and the little asses considered they had done a fair day's work. So the girls got down to ease them.

And I suppose little Neri had spied us coming. He ever had an eye on all things outside as well as inside the workshop. For we had hardly started to climb when I saw a white figure coming lightly and swiftly down the path to meet us.

"It is Jesus," I said. "He comes to welcome you. They saw us from the workshop."

And presently he met us, with Tobias jumping up beside him. He kissed me warmly on the cheek and said, "God has sped you happily, Little Azor. And these are your cousins," and he gave a welcoming hand to each of the girls.

"This is Zerah," I said, "And this is Zoe," and I felt like one who shares his chiefest treasure with his friend.

He looked sweetly and straightly at each of them, with the deep stars in his eyes, and said gently, " ' The Rising of Light,' and ' Life '. You are surely well named. Welcome to your new home! May God give you great happiness amongst us!"

And Zerah said softly, " Amen!"

And then they stood for a full minute, he and she, looking deep into one another's eyes, and I was glad, for I knew they would love one another, and they were such a noble pair.

Then we climbed on and up after the asses; and Mary, his mother, came out to greet them, and my mother too, came running down, and they all kissed one another, and the two girls were made very happy by the warmth of their greeting, and their faces showed it.

CHAPTER XII

OF NOBLE LOVERS

THE coming of Zerah and Zoe was one of the happiest things that ever happened to us, and I can never be grateful enough for it.

It was my mother's gracious thought, and we all shared in the benefit of it, and she by no means least. She loved them as if they had been her own, and they repaid her in full.

With three to share it, the housework was no longer a toil but a matter of joyous activities, spiced with much talk and laughter. A happier family could not have been found.

Of an evening, when the day's work was done, and their three spindles twirled merrily and ceaselessly as they sat outside in the cool of the sunset, very often Mary would come along from the other house and bring her spinning too, and there was for me no higher joy than to sit and listen and watch them. For I was assured in my own mind that the world had never held four more gracious and beautiful women.

As often as he could Jesus would come along too, with Tobias at his heels, and would sit and talk, and tell us stories which sometimes slowed the twirl of the spindles, so absorbing were they.

And he liked to get the others talking—which indeed needed no incitement as a rule, for when he was not there their tongues rippled on like merry brooks in spring time.

But when he was there I noticed that Zerah and Zoe were more given to listening than to talking, and Zerah especially.

Zoe would at times break spiritedly into their talk, and offer and maintain her opinions with sparkling face and lively eyes, and we would listen and watch her with enjoyment. But Zerah would sit quietly working, listening to everything, enjoying everything, and comprehending us all in the gaze of her dark eyes. Beautiful eyes they were. Always when I watched them I thought of the Pools of Heshbon on a starry night.

When Jesus talked, in that rich, tuneful voice of his, which seemed to play upon the strings of one's heart, her eyes would dwell upon him intently at times, and at times would settle on the distant hills. But I, at all events, knew that every fibre of her beautiful body, and of her soul, was strung to its uttermost to miss no slightest perception of what he meant. For at times his talk was simple enough for any to understand, but at other times, simple though it might sound, it was charged with meaning which grew and grew upon one and disclosed itself only by degrees.

Zerah remained for me just as I had thought of her that first day I saw her at Kedesh—something almost too wonderful for this common

workaday world of ours. She was, as a woman,
what Jesus was to me as a man, something quite
above and beyond one's ordinary ken, dear beyond
words, but quite recognisably above one, and
compassing heights and depths quite beyond
one.

With Zoe I never felt so. She was a year
younger than myself and still at times looked up
to me, which occasioned me great joy and satisfaction. There is surely no more certain way to
one's heart than a little loving admiration.

She was of a very bright and lively nature, and
in the genial home atmosphere I watched her
daily expanding like a flower. She was quick and
clever too in all the housework—as indeed Zerah
was no less, but Zoe's bird-like activities attracted
one's admiring attention, while Zerah's quiet
grace accomplished quite as much but passed
almost unnoticed.

It was a great joy to me that they found such
favour in Jesus's eyes. He had with all women a
way that raised them in their own esteem ; for
they all felt the high and deep respect in which
he held them ; and instinctively, I suppose, they
tried to live up to his belief in them.

I had seen it in his converse with the women of
the village, even when we were only doing their
repairs or taking their instructions for what they
wanted done. Every woman he spoke to went
about her daily tasks with a larger spirit because
she had felt the reverence in which one man
held her.

And, if that was so with outsiders, how much more with those of his intimate circle.

I have said that four more gracious and beautiful women it would not have been possible to find. He loved all gracious and beautiful things, and as we sat in the sunset with them his eyes would dwell on them with delight.

And longest and most lovingly, I came to notice in course of time, they loved to linger on our Zerah, and that was not to be wondered at, for no more surpassingly beautiful a thing to look at could he have found anywhere.

Mary and my mother had, in unusual measure, the rich matronly beauty of early middle life. They had both seen about five-and-thirty years,— they were roses opened to the sun.

Zoe, the joy—and at times now the torment— of my anxious heart, was young and girlish still in all her delightful ways. She was a rosebud unfolding day by day.

Zerah, in her maidenly reserves and unfathomable heights and depths, was like a tall white opening lily, whose snowy petals still ward the golden heart within.

It was Jesus himself so spoke of her one day as we passed a clump of lilies by the roadside. He stopped and reverently touched one, and stood gazing down into it with delight. And then he said, very softly, as if it was but his thought that spoke, "No earthly queen was ever robed like these, nor had such grace and beauty. . . . They make me think of Zerah . . . pure white and heart of gold " . . . and presently he went slowly and thoughtfully on his way and for a space was silent—thinking, I was sure, of Zerah.

Yes, his eyes loved to dwell upon her, for he loved all things gracious and beautiful. And as the months passed and he came to know her still better, his eyes seemed to seek her at once when he joined us and to rest upon her most of the time. And though his talk was for us all it seemed to me chiefly for her.

I could see that she was conscious of his look, even when her eyes were on her work or on the distant hills. For at such times the calm, sweet face would glow softly with a touch of heavenly colour akin to that of the setting sun, but it came from within and was sent there by her heart. And it always made me think how well she was named—Zerah, the Rising of Light.

And at times, moved by something he was saying, the great dark eyes would rise quietly and meet his and their souls seemed to speak to one another.

If she was not there when he came and sat down among us, I could see that he felt something awanting, and his heart was not satisfied till she came.

Now the understanding of all this came to me, not of any natural intelligence on my part, but simply because I myself was feeling in that same way towards Zoe, and I suppose it quickened me to perceive the same in him.

And in the assurance that it would make him

feel as happy and uplifted as it did me—though I hoped without those occasional torments of doubt which Zoe at times afflicted me with—I was glad.

They were such a wonderful pair, and, as it seemed to me, so absolutely made for one another. When, sometimes of an evening, we four wandered up the hill, he with Zerah and I with Zoe, I would trip at times and stumble because I could not take my eyes off them, and Zoe would laugh and call me 'Clumsy-foot.' But, really, she rejoiced as I did in the growing friendship between them.

" Yes," she would say, with many wise nods of her lively little head, " I am glad. Zerah is the most beautiful girl in the world. And he is surely the most wonderful man. And he is beautiful too. Has there ever been anyone like him ? "

" Never ! " I said vehemently, with all the devotion of my hero-worship. " He is far above all the men of Nazaret and, I should think, of all the world."

But I must not let you think that all his evenings were spent in our company. I have told about them at length because of the joy we had in them, and as I was there I could tell about them.

But there were many times when we sat hoping he might come and he did not. And we missed him. We felt something awanting. The glow of the sunset was not so bright and our talk seemed commonplace.

For as time went on he went oftener and oftener up to the hill-top alone, with the weight of many things in his face and in his step. And sometimes, though not very often, he would not even have Tobias with him. And then poor little Tobias would sit among us looking wistfully towards the hill, shifting restlessly from one foot to another, and wondering, I think, what he had done to be left behind. He could not understand that there were occasions in his master's life when even a dearly-loved dog might be in the way.

Then too, there were many evenings—too many for us—when the neighbours would come up to the workshop to discuss some news or to wrangle over some dispute, and he would go into all they required of him as though nothing else mattered. But I am as sure that he would very much sooner have been up above with us as I am that he never allowed the smallest sign of it to appear to the neighbours.

Through the still evening air we would hear their voices down there droning on and on, and sometimes growing loud and shrill in dispute, and Zerah would watch disappointedly for them to go. But very often they would stay till it was night, and then as often as not he would go away up the hill to ponder things in the quiet.

For the littleness—and worse—of his fellows lay heavy on him, and the men of Nazaret were very narrow and sometimes very crooked—like the streets in the lower part of Ptolemais—and sometimes even he could not let light into them.

There are some people whose absolute straight-forwardness is accepted by all without ever a doubt. Not very many perhaps, at least among us. For we are a self-seeking and over-reaching race, and our men of Nazaret were probably not much worse than the rest—ready to swear any-thing to clinch a bargain or gain an advantage.

But, just here and there, one lighted on a man whose word one would no more dream of doubting than one would doubt the sweetness and brightness of the morning sunshine.

Jesus ben Joseph was like that. Even the most perverse among us recognised that his ' Yea ' meant yea, and his ' Nay ' meant nay, without any other word or oath to back it up. They felt that anything in the nature of a lie, even in them-selves, was hateful to him, and in himself utterly unthinkable. One felt that he would die sooner than swerve by one iota from what he believed to be right and truth.

And I think it was that that gave him such a standing in all their disputes and discussions. They recognised that, above everything, he stood for Right and Truth, and had no end of his own to serve, as they at all times had.

As I have said, when he came down from his vigils on the hill, as a rule he showed no signs of weariness, but tackled the work in hand as if he had found new strength up there.

Yet, as time passed, I perceived that in him

which was quite beyond me. I loved him very dearly, and the eyes of love perceive things beneath the surface.

At times his thoughts were so deep and long that he spoke no word for an hour at a time, and his face was intent and absorbed though his hands worked on with unfailing certainty and skill. At such times neither Tobias and his mouse, nor the birds that he loved, could divert him from his thoughts. And much I wondered what was working within him.

His mother was greatly concerned about him. That look of—what was it ?—wondering expectancy — suspense — apprehension — appeal — that I had always been conscious of in her sweet eyes and face seemed to me to grow more pronounced in these days. And with them all was an immense solicitude which she could not hide, strive as she might.

He was very gentle and tender with her, but I do not think she obtained any enlightenment from him, or surely she would have told me when we talked of the matter.

What was working in him was—I know it now —too vast and too sacred for any discussion of it, even with his mother. And perhaps he himself was at this time only as yet beginning to understand, and even then but dimly, all that it meant.

CHAPTER XIII

OF HIS WAYS WITH MEN

As my mind wanders back along these old tracks, this happening and that starts up and appeals to me, for now I recognise them as forerunners of what came after.

I remember well how old Amos ben Rhesa—the astute old man who discovered the treasure in the field he had stripped himself to buy—came toiling up the steep path to the workshop one afternoon, and his face was sad and heavy.

He had not gone to Kaphar-Nahum, as he had thought of doing, but had bought more land and built a larger house and lived in much comfort just outside the village.

" It is Amos ben Rhesa," said Neri, long before we had noticed him. Neri's eyes missed nothing outside.

And when the old man drew near, Jesus went a little way down the path to meet him. He had doubtless heard the village talk, and guessed why he had come. He drew the trembling old arm within his own, and led him in, and seated him in a shady corner with his back to the wall. Then he went quietly on with his work and waited till the old man recovered his breath.

And presently old Amos, leaning heavily forward on his staff, said, "You and your father Joseph were always wiser than most, young Jesus, and your advice is generally sound. Tell me now what you would do in my case."

"Tell me, father, and I will gladly help if I can," said Jesus gently.

"You know I became rich through finding that treasure. . . . Sometimes I have wished it still below the ground. . . . For my boy Judah took it into his head that he must see the world. You remember him. He was at school with you.

"He was my dearest one, and when he asked for his portion I gave it to him. It was not wise perhaps, but it was hard to refuse him.

"He was young and high-spirited, and all his life he had been cooped up in Nazaret. It was but natural he should wish to see life. . . . Well, he went, and I have missed him sorely. Jotham has stayed with me and manages things for me. . . . But he is not Judah. . . .

"And now I have bad news of Judah. He has wasted his share in a young man's follies, and Jotham is hot against him. . . It breaks my heart to think of him in want. . . . He never knew want at home. . . . Shall I send for him to come home, or shall I leave him to himself, as Jotham advises ? What would you say ? "

And Jesus asked quietly, "Have you heard from Judah himself ? "

"Not one word since he went. It has troubled me sorely."

"Adversity is sometimes the best school-master, father. It may teach him what he never would have learned otherwise. It may bring him to himself. When it does he will recall your love for him and all you did for him. Then, if he has learned his lesson, his heart will turn to you, and he will come home and beg your for-giveness. He may be the better man for his suffering."

"We have thought he would probably come home. Jotham——"

"Your own heart will guide you better than Jotham, father. If he comes, asking your for-giveness——"

"Oh that he may! How I will rejoice in him! My heart aches for the sight of him. Ah me!—if I saw him coming I would run to meet him."

"We will pray that he may come, father; and if he does, greet him as your heart bids you," and presently the old man went home, slowly and heavily, for he was full of years and sorrows, but happier than when he came, because his mind was made up and he hoped to see his son again.

Another time I remember Dathan, the mason, who had started in the village after Uncle Joda died, and for whom we had done a great deal of work, fitting doors and cupboards in the houses he had built, coming up in much distress.

He was a fair workman but not a good man of business. He had lost money on some of his jobs, especially on the big new house he put up for Amos ben Rhesa. It was on the hillside, and Dathan had not gone down for his foundations as deep as Uncle Joda would have done. The winter storms undermined it somewhat, and he had been put to much trouble and expense to make it good.

He was rather easy-going with his debtors too, and never liked to press a man, and some took advantage of him.

His wife, and his little daughter Ruth, a very pretty child and the apple of his eye, had both been ill, and he found himself in debt and did not know which way to turn. He owed us, I suppose, more than anyone, and he came up in great trouble about it.

Jesus listened to him sympathetically, with those penetrating eyes of his looking through and through him.

And when Dathan had ended his tale and stood looking forlornly at him—I can see it as if it were but yesterday—Jesus smiled at him and picked up a curly shaving of cedar and said, " See now, Dathan !—here is our bill against you . . . and now——" he crumpled the cedar-shaving into fragments and threw it behind him—" it is gone. Let it trouble you no more. Better times will come."

And Dathan dropped on to his knees and cried like a child, which is a sore thing to see in a grown man.

When he had gone away comforted, I remember I said to Jesus, " You will never make money

at that rate, Jesus " ;—and the joyous laugh with
which he answered, " We have made more than
money to-day, Little Azor. We have lifted a
weight from a worthy man and given him fresh
heart."

As I have said, he still at times called me
" Little Azor," though by now I prided myself
on being fully as tall as himself, but I never could
claim his gracious mien, which made him note-
worthy in whatever company he was.

Many such things come back to me. A great
book could not contain the half of them.

I remember Naggai coming up, not long after
Dathan's visit, and with a similar plea. We had
done a lot of work for him, propping up his
house which was old and in bad condition, and
making it weather-proof and habitable. Jesus
kept urging him to seek a safer one, but he always
said he could not afford it.

And Tobias hid himself among the shavings in
a dark corner as soon as he saw him coming, as he
always did.

Jesus listened quietly to what he had to say,
with his eyes fixed gravely on his face. And when
he had done, he said quietly, " It can wait, Naggai.
We never press any man. Pay when you are
able," and Naggai went, thinking in his heart, I
fear, that, since it was left to him to decide, the
time might be long of coming.

" He could pay if he would," I said, as Jesus
picked Tobias out of the shavings and comforted
him.

" Perhaps he will," said Jesus quietly.

And presently Neri came up the path from the village, where he had been sent on a message, and he was grinning more broadly even than usual.

" Wherefore laughest thou so, little son ? " asked Jesus, smiling at his mirth.

" It was Naggai down yonder. He had old Eliakim by the beard and was wagging him as if he were a goat, and shouting, ' What about that paschal lamb you had from me, old son of a dog ? When am I going to see my money for it ? '— And old Eliakim's mouth waggled and waggled— just like an old goat he was," and Neri chuckled again at the thought of it.

But when I looked at Jesus's face it was grave and sad. He patted little Tobias, and kissed him on the head, and set him down, and went on with his work, and he spoke little all the rest of that day.

But, though many of the older folk there were quarrelsome and unneighbourly among themselves, it was always a joy to go down into the village with him, to do some job at one of their houses, even though we knew the payment might be delayed or not forthcoming at all.

For always the children of the house came running as soon as they saw the carpenter coming, and called to their friends that he was there. And they would all gather round him, with joyous shouts and sparkling eyes and faces full of expectation, and would laugh and joke with him, and call on him for stories as we worked. And out of his head and his heart he would spin them the most delightful little tales, some of them facts and many of them fancies, but all as delicately wrought and finished as a piece of his own carved work, and mostly with a little lesson in them which the pretty story would pin so firmly into their minds that they never could forget it.

He had a wonderful gift that way, and enjoyed the telling as much as they enjoyed the hearing. I wish I could recall some of them, but they were very many, and my mind at that time was very full of my own concerns, which were all centred on Zoe. I got many a gash in those days, through Zoe's sparkling face dancing about between me and my work.

CHAPTER XIV

OF HIS GRIEF AT THE LOSS OF HIS FRIEND

ANOTHER thing that I shall never forget as long as I live, was his grief at the death of little Tobias.

The little fellow had been his constant companion ever since that day, five years before, when he had saved him from Naggai's cruel hanging.

He followed his master everywhere, and by his meekness and absolute devotion had woven himself round his heartstrings.

When I came in that afternoon and found him lying in Jesus's arms, limp and spent, and panting hard for breath, my heart sank as it would not have done for many of our neighbours.

For I knew all that he was to Jesus and how dearly they loved one another. Mary was there too, and she was crying quietly.

Jesus held him as tenderly as he would have held a baby, and now and again little Tobias would turn his heavy little eyes, bright no longer, up to the sad, loving face that was bent over him, and would make an effort to lick it. And when he no longer had the strength, Jesus bent down and let him lick it and kissed him lovingly in return.

The poor little fellow lay looking up into the

sorrowful face of his friend. It was the last
thing he saw. Then he made one more effort to
kiss it but sank back, and as the beloved face bent
down to him again, he gave one little sigh, and
stretched himself out, and was gone from us.

"Faithful unto death. . . . My little loved
one!" I heard Jesus whisper. Then he kissed
the quiet little head once more, and his eyes were
sad and full of tears.

In the evening light, in which they two had so
often gone up there together, Jesus carried him
away up the hill and buried him there, but we
never knew where.

He came down in the dawn next morning, and
his face was calm and strong. But he missed his
little friend sorely, and many times in the following days he would look suddenly down and round
the workshop, and I knew he was looking for
Tobias.

He had been with us just about five years and
was loved by all of us, but by none so well as his
master.

We could only suppose that down in the village
he had picked up something that poisoned him,
but we had not the knowledge or the experience
to discover what it was or how to defeat it.

The first time Jesus came to sit with us after
Tobias's death, I heard Zerah murmur softly as
she greeted him, "We are all so very sorry," and
he said quietly, "It is always sad to lose a faithful
friend, but happy are they who have nothing to
reproach themselves with when it is too late."

And then, as he sat among us, he told us many things about Tobias's funny little ways and how he had endeared himself to him, and how he missed him every minute of the day. And he said, sadly and thoughtfully, " If we could all be as faithful and as loving as little Tobias how much happier the world would be ! "

CHAPTER XV

Of a Fight he Fought and Won

I was wildly in love with Zoe, and when she consented to marry me my cup was full to the brim.

For her sister Zerah my feeling was, as it had been from the first time I saw her in her house at Kedesh, and as it has been ever since, one of intensest admiration, adoration almost, such as the Greeks and others might feel towards their goddesses.

·But, while I loved her dearly, I always felt her very far above me in every way. I would no more have thought of loving her in the way I loved Zoe than I would have thought of loving the sun or the moon.

She was to me a being apart, of a loftier and finer nature than any I had ever met—yes, to me different even from my mother or Joseph's Mary. They may have been even finer and sweeter, but I was young and they were nearing middle-age, or so it seemed to me.

And that feeling of aboveness—not aloofness, for Zerah was ever intimately one of ourselves, and most loving and sisterly in all our doings—and my feeling of reverence for her grew greater still, as I shall tell you.

Between my best of friends and this my dearest
of sisters I could see growing up a love which
rejoiced me greatly.

A nobler pair the world has never seen—of
that I am certain. Bodily and mentally—and as
I may now believe, spiritually—they seemed
meant for one another. And yet nothing seemed
to come of it, and I was sorely puzzled.

That Jesus rejoiced in her—in her grace and
beauty, in her sweetness of heart, and loftiness of
soul, was apparent to all of us. His eyes loved
to dwell upon her. The sight of her seemed to
help and soothe him when other people's troubles
and waywardnesses lay heavy on him.

And yet at times—and that it was that puzzled
me so—he seemed almost to shun her. Often I
could see she looked for him to come and he came
not, and my heart was sore for her, for I knew
what it meant to her.

And at this time the burden of his thoughts
was such that for hours on end we would work
side by side with scarce a word between us.

I had very early learned when he wanted to be
alone with himself, and at such times I forbore
from troubling him. Yet, if a neighbour came
in to discuss his affairs with him or to ask his
advice, Jesus would give all his mind to him, and
would devote himself to the matter as if it were
the only thing in the world that needed him.

I never could have done that, and many a time
I would have liked to send them about their
business with a sharp word, when I saw them

adding the weight of their foolish little quarrels
to all that he was already bearing.

But he was not like that, and none of them ever
lacked from him the kindliest consideration.—
Unless, indeed, one of them came with the inten-
tion of deceiving him, and then he went back
smaller than he came and knowing himself very
much better—but never knew how barely he
escaped from me the biting word, or even the
kick, I itched to administer.

Jesus's thoughts in those days seemed almost
too much for him. At times he would straighten
up from the bench and stand gazing meditatively
out over the plain towards Hermon, and then
perhaps he would silently raise his arms as though
he were praying for guidance or help, and as they
sank again he would bend to the bench and get on
with the work more intently than ever.

And I wondered if it was thought of Zerah and
doubt of her love for him that was troubling him.
I knew myself what torment that could be to a
man, but I did not see how he could have a
moment's uncertainty on that head. I had none.
Zerah, I knew, loved him, body, soul, and spirit,
absolutely.

He was suffering. I could see it. I would
have done anything I could to help him. And
once I did venture—but only once.

" Jesus," I burst out, one such time when we
were alone in the workshop, " are you in doubt
about Zerah ? She loves you with her whole
heart and soul. I am sure of it."

And he turned and looked at me with those deep eyes of his which seemed to look right through one, but now they were heavy with the stress of his feeling, heavy almost to tears, it seemed to me. Just then they were very like those other eyes, which always made me think of the Pools of Heshbon.

And he said softly, " That is how a man would be loved, Little Azor," and he patted me gently on the shoulder, as who would say, " But there are things that even well-meaning little boys cannot quite understand," and he went on with his work.

But that night he and Zerah went up the hill together in the sunset, hand in hand as lovers should, and my heart rejoiced greatly. And when Zoe would have had us go too, I restrained her and we went off by another path.

The moon was up when Zerah came in and went quietly to her own room. I got but a glimpse of her face as she passed, but I can see it yet, after all these years. That is perhaps because I have seen it so often just the same since then.

It was calm and quiet, but strangely radiant and uplifted, as though the soul within her had been kindled into heavenly flame and could not but show through.

We saw her no more that night, and it was many years later before I heard from her own lips what passed between them on the hill-top.

When I went to the workshop in the morning, Jesus was not there, and Mary, when she heard me at work, came in, with that apprehensive look strong in her sweet face, and said, " Azor, he has

not come home. Do you think anything can
have befallen him up there ? "

" He loves to stop up above when he has much
to think on," I said.

" But he has always come down before."

" If he does not come I will go seek him," and
she sighed, with a little catch in the breath.

But as the sun climbed high and the morning
passed, I began to grow anxious myself. He had
never lingered up there so long as this, and we had
some pressing work on hand.

I put my head in through the house-door and
said, " I will go seek him, Mother. But no harm
has befallen him, I am sure. So don't be
troubled."

" But I am," she said, and she looked it.

I went quickly up the path he usually took, but
he was not on our hill, and it was quite a while
before I found him on the top of one of the
further hills.

He was lying prone, on his face, in a curious
attitude,—his arms stretched out in front of him,
his head sunk in between them, as though indeed
he had fallen asleep while praying.

At first I thought some ill had come to him,
but then I saw by the slow regular movement of
his sides that he really was fast asleep.

From my knowledge of him and love for him I
was sure that he must have been unusually weary
to fall asleep like that. And as sleep is the best
restorative for an over-tired man I forbore to
wake him. I gathered some branches and made

a little shelter over him from the heat of the sun, and sat down and waited.

It was a long time, and seemed longer, before he made the slightest movement. Then I saw, by the lessening of his breathing, that he was awake.

He lifted his head from between his arms and lay gazing out over the plains. Then his arms rose in a gesture of entreaty and he murmured, " Eloï ! Eloï ! Eloï ! "

It was but a whisper, but in some strange way it seemed to my heart to be compounded of supplication, penitence, submission, and it sent a lump into my throat. He was suffering, though how and why I could not tell.

His head sank down again and a convulsive sob shook him, almost a shudder.

Then, after a while, he gave a deep sigh and sat straight up, as one who has suffered a weakness and suddenly determines to brace himself to strength again.

My screen of branches fell about him. He looked round and saw me sitting there.

" It is you, Little Azor," he said quietly. " And you covered me from the sun. . . . It was good of you."

" Your mother was in distress about you, Jesus. She begged me to seek you."

" Let us go down," he said, and as we went he leaned on my shoulder, a thing he had never done before.

He did not touch his tools that day, but, after eating, sat quietly in the shade, and his face and his attitude were those of one who has gone through heavy fighting and has won through,— but at sore cost.

I wondered much how things stood between him and Zerah, for I was eager for their happiness; and the first time they met I could not but watch them closely.

But I could not make anything of it. That they had talked their matter out, I was sure; and that they understood one another, and I was glad. But I could get no further.

She met his loving gaze, when he came in, with an answering gaze of most perfect love and under-standing. Her beautiful face was luminous with the feeling that was in her, and—have I dreamt it or deceived myself?—it seems to me that never after that did she quite lose that exalted and uplifted look and that serene and supreme con-fidence in her eyes.

It was many years before I came to any proper understanding of the matter. But through those years Zerah lived with us, and she was as an angel of light in our house, and in many another house as well.

From that time I could not but notice how often Jesus would rest for a moment from his work, and stand gazing out into the far-away. And I wondered if he was thinking of Zerah.

But now I know that it was of greater things still —things which I could not have understood and which indeed he as yet understood but dimly himself.

CHAPTER XVI

OF THE MAKING OF THE SEAMLESS ROBE

By careful management Mary had saved out of
her household expenses a certain sum of money,
as most good housewives do. And she must have
done it steadily for a very long time, adding
farthing to farthing, and hoarding them carefully,
with one special object in view.

For when she had enough she bought with it a
quantity of unusually fine Egyptian flax through a
merchant who went at times as far as Tyre. And
well I remember Jesus joking her when it came.

"Now she will outshine all the neighbours,"
he laughed. "Won't they stare when she goes
into the synagogue the first time with it on.
They'll think we've dug up a treasure like Amos
ben Rhesa, and will all come wanting to borrow
money from us."

"What am I going to make then?" asked Mary,
with dancing eyes.

"A tsaiph of a certainty. Flax such as that
would be wasted on anything less."

"We shall see," said Mary, hugging her happy
secret.

She used to spin it of an evening when we all

118

sat talking in the sunset. And the sun seemed to linger over the Western hills, to watch her sweet intent face and the loving touch of her slender fingers as they twisted the fine soft fibre.

We all loved the feel of that beautiful flax, and fingered with enjoyment the smoothness and evenness of the thread she spun out of it. And then we watched with ever-increasing interest the final weaving.

To us men it was still a mystery what it was to be, but I think my mother and the girls guessed. Though the garment Mary was making was not like any of the ordinary ones.

" It's not a tsaiph," said Jesus, with a puzzled face, as he watched the loom one day. " And it's not a milpachath ,and it's not a maatapha. So what can it be ? Is it some new fashion you've invented, Little Mother ? "

" It's as old as the hills and as new as a mother's love," she smiled, and then told him the secret before the loom should give it away. " What about a meil for my big son ? "

" A meil !—for me ? . . . But it's too fine and good for me, Mother. It's fit for a Queen's wearing. Yes, it is fit even for you yourself."

" Or a King's," she said, with a quick smile, " and are you not my King ? "

" You do me great honour, Mother mine. But it will be almost too beautiful to wear. I've never seen such a meil before."

" No—you see, as it was for you I wanted it different. So I'm making it all of a piece—

without ever a seam in it,—no stitching up the side for me,—for you ! "

" It's wonderful—the most wonderful meil that ever was made. I shall be robed like a King indeed."

" As you should be," said his mother, with that far-away look in her eyes—the look I had so often noticed there,—of love and longing, and expectation, and puzzled apprehension.

It was no easy matter for her on her small loom, but she wrought steadily at it, and I am sure enjoyed every minute she gave to that labour of love.

Often, in pauses of our work outside, we would hear the regular clap-clap-clap-clap of the loom, and the ceaseless swift rush of the shuttle within, and Jesus would look at me with a happy smile, as much as to say, " Was there ever such a mother as mine ? "

When the first tunic was finished, and carefully washed and bleached and fulled, she made him put it on and come and show it to us.

And truly it was the most wonderful meil we had any of us ever seen. For Mary had wrought upon it, in pale-blue thread—just the tint of the morning sky, which was always her favourite colour—some of the delicate and beautiful embroidery which she had learned in Egypt during her sojourn there, and it looked almost too good to wear.

It fitted him perfectly, and both she and he were very proud of it—he, for the love she had woven into it and she, for the joy it gave him, and for the satisfaction which good work always gives to the doer of it.

" I will wear your meil as long as I live, Little Mother," Jesus said, as he kissed her tenderly. " There never was one like it before."

" I will make another," said Mary happily, " so that you will always have a change. And truly meils like that should last you a life-time, for there is nothing in it but the very best. I've made sure of that. . . . And," turning him round and round admiringly, " it fits you well. What a big son it is ! . . . I wore it myself for an hour but it was much too big for me. I felt quite lost in it."

And Jesus kissed her warmly again. For among us, one can show no greater love and esteem than to give or lend to a friend a garment of honour which one has worn oneself.

" Your love spun it and wove it and has worn it," he said joyously. " And always it shall tell me of you and your love and make my heart warm."

And always, when the meils were finished, he wore one of them, and their pure soft whiteness sat well on him and added not a little to the sweet dignity of his appearance.

One could well imagine a special virtue in his garments, for they drew both from himself and from her who made them. And they were ever fragrant with the love that overflowed from both their hearts, and with the sweet scent of the rosemary leaves which Mary always folded up in the one that was not being worn.

Her two great bushes of rosemary grew just outside the workshop and were her very great delight. The sweet clean smell of them, mingled with that of fresh-cut cedar and pine and oak, filled all the place and always helped us much in our work.

CHAPTER XVII

OF THE COMING OF THE COUSINS

I PASS over much, or this chronicle would know no end.

More changes came. Zoe and I were married, and Mary and Jesus of course graced our wedding-feast.

We were all humble folk together, but the presence of Mary and Jesus and Zerah and my mother were enough to lift that wedding-feast above the ordinary and make it memorable, and the neighbours felt it so.

We built another room on to the house and settled down to a very happy home life. The workshop kept us busy all day, and in the evening we forgathered in one or other of our houses, and span and talked and listened, and were contented and happy.

Then late one night, when we had all gone to bed, there came a knocking on our door, and, tired with a hard day's work, I was loth to rise and answer it.

"Let them knock," I said. "It can be only some stranger."

But the knocking continued, and then I heard

a voice calling me by name, and I sprang out of bed and ran to open.

It was Jesus from next door.

"Too bad, Little Azor, and I am sorry to spoil your sleep," he said. "But we have un-expected visitors down there—my cousins, James and Simon and Jude, and they are famished and we have not enough for them. Lend me all the bread you can spare till to-morrow."

"All we have," I said.

"Nay—what you can spare. My mother will bake again as soon as it is light."

So, after a word with Zoe, I got him three loaves and some small cakes, and he thanked me warmly and went off with them. And I went back to bed wondering who these cousins could be.

John, the hairy boy of the hill-tops, I remem-bered well, but these were evidently some other cousins of whom I had never heard.

My mother was still trying in her mind to settle who they were, when I went down to the workshop and found them there, sitting talking with Mary and Jesus, who was already hard at work.

"I will take up the loaves and thank your mother within the hour, Azor," said Mary. "Mine are almost ready. It was good of her to let us have them. These are my sister's sons— that is James . . . Simon . . . Jude. Joses and his three sisters and their mother are on the way. We are wondering where to put them all."

Then my mother came in, full of curiosity

concerning the newcomers, whose identity had
been troubling her all night.

"They are the sons of my sister Mary, who
married Clopas of Beth-Shunam," said Mary.
"He has died, and Mary wants to come and live
with us, though how we are to manage it I do
not see."

There was much talk about it all day, while
Jesus and I got on with our work, which could not
wait on family arrangements. But he listened
quietly and dropped in a helpful word when
chance offered.

I could well imagine his own feelings regarding
this invasion. It meant an end and a new
beginning—an end of the quiet secluded life with
his mother, which had been, and had done, so
much for him—a new beginning with a crowd of
unknown cousins who might or might not be
congenial and fit in.

These three, indeed, seemed inoffensive enough.
James was, I judged, about the same age as Jesus;
Simon, some years younger; Jude, younger still.
Joses, whom we had not yet seen, came between
James and Simon; and there were also three
girls. These, with their mother, Clopas's Mary,
would reach Nazaret that day or the next. The
three had been sent on ahead to make arrangements.

But whatever his own feelings in the matter,
Jesus was the last one could ever think of allowing
them to stand in the way of being of service to
anyone in need.

I gathered, from the talk, that Clopas had not been a successful man—except in the production of a family too large for his means. He had, indeed, obeyed the old injunction given to Noah. He had been fruitful and multiplied, and had replenished the earth, but the earth had repaid him but scantily.

Mary saw all the difficulties, but her good heart would not let her refuse her sister such help as was possible. And after much discussion it was settled that extra rooms of wood should be erected against the house, and they should all live together—the boys helping as they could in the workshop or elsewhere in the village, and the girls assisting Mary in the house.

Fortunately it was summer, and the erection of the rooms and their simple furnishings presented no great difficulties, and we all set to work on them at once.

The rest of the large family arrived next day, and despite the additional trouble it was bound to cause her, Mary was glad to see her sister and gave her very warm welcome.

Clopas's Mary seemed to me—to us, for we discussed them all at home, as was natural—very different from Jesus's Mother. They were sisters, indeed, but of very different mould—different both in appearance and in character.

The bearing of seven children and the rearing of them on scanty means, with all the inevitable anxieties entailed thereby, had left Clopas's Mary a rather weary woman. She had had some of her sister's good looks, but the cares of life had clouded them, and, without knowledge, you would not have suspected their close kinship.

She was worn and tired-looking and the more so with the long hot journey—but she seemed gentle and amiable, and very grateful for having reached a home at last where there was possibility of a decent living.

The boys and girls were all strong and healthy, in spite of, or by reason of, their simple life and scanty faring, and were all ready to do their share of the work.

On the whole I thought we were not likely to suffer much from the invasion—except Jesus, and for him I was inclined to fear that that crowded house would be less of a home than it had been.

But he had always the hills, and after the others came he spent more and more of his off-times up there, and always came back the better for it.

The newcomers very soon came to look up to him as did all who really knew him, and his most quietly expressed wish was as the law in that house. Later on, as they grew older, their various personalities asserted themselves, but in the meantime they did their best not to obtrude themselves upon him over-much.

They recognised, I think, as we others long since had done, that he was a man apart, different from the ordinary run of men, though how and why they understood no more than we did.

I remember well the first time the boys came up to our house. They met Zoe first, and were

so struck with her that it was a long time before
they could find their tongues.

They were just beginning to feel less dumb
before her when Zerah and my mother came out
with their spinning. Then speech failed them
again, and they simply sat and gazed at our
beautiful Zerah as if she were not of this earth.
She did her best, gently and graciously, to put
them at their ease, but it took several visits
before they plucked up courage to talk to her as
an ordinary mortal, as they did to Zoe and my
mother.

When Jesus came up one night to sit and talk
with us, and he and Zerah greeted one another
with that look of perfect trustful love and understanding which always passed between them, I
have no doubt the elder boys drew their own
conclusions. I am sure they worshipped her from
afar, for their faces and their voices when they at
times mustered courage to speak to her, told
their own tales.

In time they all settled down into their own
places. James, who had learned some carpentering, assisted us in the workshop, and before
long, Jude, the youngest of them, joined us there
also. Simon was good with animals and got a
place with old Peleg down in the village—he who
did the carrying trade to and from the Lake—
whose asses I had hired when I went up to Kedesh
for Zerah and Zoe, not knowing what exceeding
good fortune awaited me there.

Peleg was growing fat and lazy, and was glad to

have a trustworthy youth to go to and fro on his business, and Simon enjoyed the traffic, and the ventures of the Great Road, and the mixing with other men.

Joses knew mason's work. He went with Dathan, down in the village, and helped him to build and repair houses. The girls, Mary, Miriam, and Salome assisted the two mothers with the housework and spun and wove with the others.

I cannot say that I was glad they had all come. Our happy fellowship of the workshop was never quite the same, though we all worked well together. But two alone can come much closer to one another than is possible when there are four. We were kept busy, but when the work was divided among four each man's share was much lightened.

Jesus still loved best his work on yokes and plows, and men still came from afar for them. He had instilled into me his own strong feeling about them and was always well pleased with those I turned out.

James and Jude were, in time, able to undertake much of the other work and the village jobs, and Jesus was freer than he had been of late for helping and advising the neighbours, who, nevertheless, found endless matters for dispute. No sooner was one trouble settled than a fresh one broke out. They were quarrelsome folk down there. The best thing I can say about them is that in most cases they accepted his view of the matter, though they never seemed to grow any wiser themselves.

He directed all our doings and neglected nothing. There were many times when I could see he was longing for the solitude of the hill-top, when, nevertheless, he remained below with us to make quite sure that all was going on right. Then when he felt himself free he would go up and would remain there for hours and sometimes all night.

The cousins wondered much and questioned me, but I could tell them no more than they could see for themselves. In the depths and heights and width of his thoughts he was as far above us as the sky is above the earth. They regarded him with wonder and awe as one beyond their understanding.

But for the accepted fact that he was wiser, and of a more equable temper, and more evenly balanced in his mind than any man they had ever met, they might have thought him a little mad. As it was, they accepted him as unusually clever, but somewhat odd in his ways, and he remained to them, as to most of us, an unsolvable puzzle.

CHAPTER XVIII

OF THE MOVE TO THE LAKE

LIFE flowed on for a time very happily with us—deep and smooth. We were enjoying a reach of the river untroubled by rocks or shallows. And then came the inevitable break.

Simon, in his journeyings to the Lake, saw much of men and the busy life of the towns, and his accounts of such kindled in the hearts of the younger folk a desire to see more of the world than Nazaret could afford them.

It was perhaps not unnatural. They were all growing up and reaching out for larger things. They were probably—nay almost certainly—looking forward to marriage and the bringing up of children. And Nazaret held but small hopes for them in such matters. And our trade, which had comfortably supported six, found twelve somewhat of a burden.

There were many discussions about it, some of which went on as we all sat in the sunset together when the day's work was done, and others no doubt among themselves in the house below.

The upshot of it all was that the joint family at last decided to remove to Kaphar-Nahum on the

Lake, where the aspirations of the eager young folk would find larger scope, and the family income would be more likely to equal the demands upon it.

For there, in addition to all the work we were accustomed to, there were boats to be mended, and many repairs to the gear of the caravans that travelled the Great Roads to Damascus and the Desert and the South—endless opportunities for work.

Thought of the boats filled me with desire to go too. I would have loved to repair boats, and perhaps build them. But my mother and Zoe had no wish for it. Our simple life on the hillside filled all their desires, and I did not press the matter.

We had two fine boys, and perhaps Zoe was right in thinking that the hillside was better for them than the plain and the towns of the Lake.

I was doubtful how Jesus would look upon the matter, but then I had to confess to myself that he was entirely above and beyond my comprehension. Whatever he thought, however, and whatever his reasons for thinking it, he raised no objection to the general wish.

Zerah, I could see, felt it keenly, though perhaps no one saw that but myself. I was so deeply interested in both him and her, and I loved them both so dearly, that anything affecting them touched me very closely.

She went about her work, indeed, with a face as calm and brave as ever, and I seemed to find

in it, more even than before, that radiance and
out-shining of an inward light which, to my eyes,
gave her the appearance of a visitor from a
better world.

I knew that whatever he decided was right in
her eyes, that she felt within her the perfect
assurance that whatever he determined was for
the best. But I knew too that when he went
her heart would go with him, and I feared the
results to herself.

But that was only because I was not capable of
understanding her yet. The heights and depths
of that large heart of hers were beyond me, as
were his.

When the great upheaval had been accomplished and they were all gone, we moved down
to the other house so that I could live alongside
my workshop. Zerah, as of right, took the room
Jesus had always occupied, and I think she found
some consolation in that.

It was to her, I am sure, a sacred place, and
the very walls spoke to her of him continually.
If their stones had had tongues—what could they
not have told her ? But perhaps, to her uplifted and love-quickened perception, they spoke
more clearly than with tongues. For spirit
speaks to spirit in ways unknown to men. This,
and more, I learned later on.

Their going made a tremendous gap in our
life. We missed them at every turn. The
quarrelsome neighbours did not come up to consult me as they used to come to Jesus—in which

they showed wisdom. It was no loss, either to them or to me—but still I missed them.

And for a time my trade suffered through folks going to Kaphar-Nahum for their yokes and plows, which was only right and natural since it was Jesus who had made them in such demand.

But in course of time, as my yokes and plows—made just as he would have made them and as carefully wrought—got known, a portion of that trade came back to me; and for the rest, as I always worked on his lines of putting my very best into all I did, I maintained my reputation as a trustworthy workman, and had quite as much as I could do with Neri's help.

But we missed them all—and most of all that calm commanding figure which used to come so quietly in among us of an evening, and by his presence, as by his talk, lifted us all above our usual selves.

As we sat now in the sunset glow we would recall the things he had said and his way of saying them. And very many times I turned to the place where he used to sit, expecting to find him there, so strong was the feeling that he was still with us.

And, indeed, when the light faded, and we still sat on in the gathering shadows, more than once I so felt him there, and caught the light of his starry eyes upon me, that I spoke to him as though he really were there, and the others laughed at my foolishness.

But there was an ache and a longing in their

laughter. And Zerah, I felt sure, understood, for she never laughed at me, but sat intent and quiet. Perhaps she also felt and saw him as I thought I did.

Twice I made the journey to the Lake to see him. But it was a whole day's travel each way, and but for the lift Simon gave me on one of Peleg's asses I could not have spared the time.

As we jogged along—at a much better pace than when I went to Kedesh, for Simon understood asses and how to get the best out of them— he told me, among many other things, some news which amused me greatly.

Two of his sisters, after all their desire for the larger life on the Lake, were coming back to Nazaret. Miriam was to marry Jotham, the son of rich old Amos ben Rhesa, who found the treasure. And Salome was to marry Eber, the son of Mattathias the corn-merchant. Mary would be the only one left at home. " But," said Simon, " she will not be at home long, for she's a pretty girl and will soon find a man to her liking."

I found them all very comfortably settled in a good-sized house on the shore of the Lake to the north of the town, and business was evidently good with them.

They seemed all well satisfied with the move ; the large courtyard was strewn with work ; there were boats drawn up on the shore for repairs ; their new neighbours had already begun to gather there of an evening to talk things over with

Jesus, and I could see that they savoured his wisdom and clear judgment as the men of Nazaret had done.

He seemed to me older, and more full of thought than ever. But his eyes were as bright and penetrating as before, his voice as round and sweet, his mien as gentle and gracious, and he showed me that our friendship had suffered nothing from our parting.

In the evening he drew me to a walk by the lake-side, just we two alone, and we talked of the old times at Nazaret.

I had given them all our news when I arrived, but now he asked more particularly :

" And Zerah ? "

" She misses you much, but she is very wonderful and angel-good. We would have missed you even more had she not been with us," and I told him how more than once I had believed him there and had even spoken to him.

" I am often there with you all in the spirit," he said quietly. " No matter how much the new duties call one it is joy at times to get back to one's old friends and the places one has loved."

" How do you find the neighbours here ? " I asked, " as quarrelsome as our Nazaret folk ? "

" Men are much the same everywhere, my Azor," he said, and there was more than a touch of sadness in his voice as he added, " More men— more sin, more sorrow, more suffering. . . . And, it might, and ought to be so different, if only they would see things rightly and think rightly about them. . . . And they could ; they could, if they would . . . if—only—they—would ! "— from which I gathered that the men of Kaphar-Nahum were no better than the men of Nazaret, and that their short-comings and overdoings were a burden to him.

" Unless an awakening comes," he said again, " they will die in their sleep. . . . And how shall it come ? . . ." But he did not answer his own question, and we paced on in silence.

Then he lifted up his arms, in the way I knew so well, and said deeply, " It is in God's hands. He will see to it."

CHAPTER XIX

OF THE COMING OF LITTLE JOHN

NOTHING could fill the place of him I had lost. But not long afterwards a new pleasure came into my life and afforded me a measure of consolation.

The upper little house, in which we had at first lived, was taken by a woman of some wealth who lived in Jerusalem.

She had one son, a boy of about ten, whose bodily health did not thrive there. She had taken our old house so that they could spend a part of each year on the hills, in the sweet strong air that came up from the sea.

She was a good woman, and my mother and Zoe and Zerah were friends with her at once. And her boy, John, took a liking for me and became to me very much what I had been to Jesus, save for the difference between us in point of age.

I often smiled to myself at sight of him sitting there among the shavings, just as I used to do. And I tried to be to him, in a small way, what Jesus had been to me

He was an unusually clever boy, his mind at times too active for his body, and that was why

they had come. While he was in Nazaret he was
to run wild and learn nothing that would trouble
his active brain too much.

As their nearest neighbours we became very
friendly—just as I had done with Jesus, and he
loved to run into the workshop and sit and chatter
there, as I had done ten, twelve years before.

I could not hope to be to him what Jesus had
been to me. But he looked up to me as many
years older and wiser than himself, and so we got
on very well together.

I naturally told him much about the friend
whose place and house I was occupying—told
him what a leader he had been to us all—and of
our rambles on the hills and adventures at the
great pool, where half of us came nigh to drowning—and much besides.

" I'd love to pray like that on the hill-top in the
dawn," said the small boy. " When will you
take me, Azor ? And to swim in that pool——"

" Can you swim ? "

" I've never tried. But he could."

" Yes, he could, but the others couldn't."

" Why couldn't they swim too ? "

" Because he doesn't know what fear is. Perhaps you do."

" I wouldn't be afraid if you were there. When
can we go ? "

" We'll see when next holiday comes."

" Well, tell me more about him. I like hearing
about him. I wish he was here still."

" So do I, little John. And so do many others.

But perhaps he'll come this way to see us some day, and I hope you'll be here when he comes."

" If I knew when he was coming I'd get my mother to wait. I'm sure she'd like him too."

" Yes, I'm sure she would. It would be a very strange person that did not. You'd love him as I do if you saw him—couldn't help it. There's something about him that makes him different from any other man I've ever met."

" What is it ? "

" You'll feel it when you meet him. I doubt if I could make you understand."

" I can understand a lot. My mother says I understand too much."

" Then maybe she will scold me if I add any more to it," I laughed.

" She tells me not to work my brain while I'm here. But I can't live if I don't work my brain."

" You're here to get strong. The stronger you get the better you will use your brain."

" Has Jesus got a very big brain ? "

" Yes, little John—a wonderful brain, and a still more wonderful heart—big enough to take you and all the rest of the world into it."

" He *must* be a big man."

" The biggest man I ever met."

" As big as the giant that David slew ? "

" Oh, very much bigger—not just in body, but in everything else that goes to the making of a man."

" He must be a very big man. Does everyone like him as much as you do, Azor ? "

" The bad ones, and those who try to deceive him, don't like him at all. I've seen him wither them with a look."

" Not really ! "—with incredulous round eyes.

" I don't mean their bodies—their hearts and their evil consciences. I've seen men go crawling down that path like beaten dogs. His eyes see right through you, and if you try to mislead him they flame and scorch."

" Did you ever try to mislead him, Azor ? "

" No, never. You see, I loved him too much, and he loved me."

" He must be a great man. I do wish I could see him," he sighed. And after a time, he said, in a way that told me he was half afraid I would laugh at him, " Azor . . . perhaps he's the Deliverer we're all waiting for. He'll have to be a very big man. They say he is coming very soon now. And I'm sure we need him badly enough. . . . I wish all the Romans could die to-night. You don't feel them here as we do in Jerusalem. Their hand is heavy on us "—which he had doubtless often heard said, for it was the general feeling of us all.

Our friendship ripened and we had many happy times together—on the hill-tops and at the pool, where in time he learned to swim all right. The Great Road and its marvels he did not care for. He saw more than enough of all that at Jerusalem.

Boy-like he recounted to his mother, Mary, all that I told him about Jesus, and she was intensely interested and questioned me much about him.

Like her boy, she had a capacious mind and was of a very enquiring disposition, and she had a very warm heart. And, like all thoughtful men and women of those days she longed and prayed for the speedy coming of the Deliverer, who should free us from the hand of Rome and set us in our rightful place at the head of the nations.

Now I have told you about this boy John, because he was my friend and a comfort to my loneliness, and later on it was from him that we learned much of what our hearts longed and ached to know of the happenings elsewhere.

John of course promptly fell in love with Zerah, who was twice his age and more. Though, indeed, she did not look it, for that pure white flame that burned within her kept her perpetually young at heart, and she seemed to us all to grow in grace and beauty with every day that passed. Her heart was so full of ever-growing love for her chosen one that it overflowed on to all whom she met.

No wonder little John fell over head and ears in love with her. He worshipped her; and though I knew he liked me well, I sometimes thought he came to sit in the workshop quite as much in hopes of seeing her as of talking to me.

But they were only with us in the hot season, and I always missed little John much when the time came for them to go back to Jerusalem.

CHAPTER XX

OF THE NEW PROPHET

OUR two boys, Azor and Zadok, were growing
strong and sturdy, and Zoe and I were rightly
proud of them, but her hands were kept very full
with them.

My carpenter's work went well. All the
neighbours had come to know that any job
entrusted to me would be well and promptly
done—to the very best of my ability, and I was
no mean workman. I had learned my craft in a
good school, and for the rest, I did my utmost in
all things to act as I believed my teacher would
have wished. For very love of him I had always
tried to be like him, and to do, as nearly as I
could, what he would have done.

Looking back now, the years seem to have sped
quickly, with no great happenings to mark them
with black stones or white.

Each Spring, young John from Jerusalem came
bursting joyously in upon us, glad to get away
from the tumultuous life of the City, and very
happy to be once more in the company of the
hill - tops and of us simple dwellers on the
slopes.

I remember well the time he came very full of the fact that he had decided to become a lawyer. That was a calling for which his active brain seemed well fitted. And there was always plenty of work for lawyers, for quarrels and disputes throve among us like weeds in a neglected garden.

But when he told me that he was busy learning a new kind of script, which would enable him to write as fast as a man could talk, I smiled at him, and looked on it as a piece of boyish exaggeration. Nevertheless, I believe he did learn it and in time was able to write at a speed little short of marvellous.

But it took him a long time, and when he was with us his mother would not have him touch it, but insisted on him running loose and giving his brain a rest.

He and his mother cannot, however, have been with us when I heard in the village the first rumour of one—a prophet or a preacher—who was making a great stir down south.

He was said to be rousing the people with his fiery talk, and they were flocking to hear him in multitudes.

When I told this at home I was surprised by the effect it had on Zerah especially. Her calm sweet face lit up. Her great eyes shone more wonderfully than ever with the feelings my news aroused in her.

" Who is it, Azor ? " she asked, with excitement she could not hide.

" No one seems to know. Some say he is

Elijah come back, and some say he is the Deliverer
we have waited for so long. Whoever he is he is
waking men up—and they need it. I'll go down
to-night and see if I can get hold of Simon.
He gets all the latest news at the Lake."

The women talked ceaselessly about the matter,
and in the evening I went down into the village
to seek Simon at Peleg's house.

But he was not there. He should have been
back from the Lake that day, but he had not come,
and Peleg was anxious about him, for with five
laden asses on the Great Road you never knew
what might happen.

They were all discussing the new prophet, and
every man had his own idea and asserted it
vociferously. But none of them knew anything
for certain.

I saw the disappointment in Zerah's eager face
when I had no news for her. I wondered much
what she was thinking. And, pondering her and
the matter generally, I arrived at the idea that
she believed the new prophet was Jesus.

That was the natural conclusion for me to
come to. But I remember, even now, how
startling it was to me.

He was the most wonderful man I had ever met,
and he was the best and dearest friend I had ever
had or could ever hope to have. But, somehow,
I had not thought of him quite in that way. . . .

I went down again the next night and found
Simon returned and full of news.

They were talking of nothing else on the Lake,

and many were going down Jordan to hear the new preacher.

"And who is he ?—Who is he ?—Who is he ? " was the constant question. But Simon only told us who he was not.

"He says himself he is not Elijah—nor the Deliverer. But he says the Deliverer is very close at hand and the Kingdom is nigh. And he calls on all to repent before it is too late."

And then, looking very pointedly at me, of all the throng that surrounded him, he said, " They say he is a wild, hairy man, and is dressed in the skins of wild beasts, and he lives in the deserts and eats nothing but honey and the fruit of the locust-tree, and he carries a long stick in his hand."

When he could get away from the rest he came along to me, and we walked apart, and he said, " Jesus told me to tell you that about him. He said you would know who he is."

"Your Cousin—John ben Zechariah ! "

"Yes . . . I do not care to tell these others. They would think I was lying or boasting. Besides it might do him no good. If they knew it was only our Cousin John, who has always been a little bit mad, they might think the less of him. For, mind you, he is doing good. He's making people think—making them think they're not as good as they ought to be, and there's no doubt about that. If his preaching makes them even a little bit better it's all to the good."

"And how is Jesus ?—and Mary ?—and all the

rest of the family ? And what does he say about
it all ? "

" They are all full of it, like everybody else. . . ."
Then he fell thoughtful for a space, and said
presently, " What Jesus thinks of it all, I do
not know. . . . You know, Azor . . . at times I
can't understand him at all. He's beyond me.
. . . He goes wandering away up into the hills,
all by himself, in that queer way of his. I know
he always used to, but it's grown upon him of
late. He's got something on his mind, that's
certain. They're all a bit worried about him at
home."

" You can trust him, Simon. He's the best
and biggest man I ever knew. And I'm quite
sure the work doesn't suffer by his going up into
the hills."

" No, I don't say it does. He's a wonderful
hand at his work, and gets through it in half the
time another would take. And yet he never
scamps it. It's always tip-top what he turns out."

" I'm quite sure he never scamps it. That's
not his way. He's the cleverest craftsman in all
Galilee and he puts his heart into all he does."

" He does that . . . and yet, they tell me, his
mind seems always full of other things. If I
was always thinking of other things I'd lose half
my beasts. Of course when one is on the Great
Road one needs all one's wits about one."

" I'm sure," I said, though it made me smile
inside, this magnifying of his own position, as
driver of Peleg's meek little asses, in comparison

with Jesus's work. I was sure he thought Jesus would find it a very different and difficult job to lead his team to and from the Lake.

" Bring us all the news you can of the new preacher, Simon," I said. " They are all anxious to hear all they can of him at home. And tell Jesus we are all longing to see him again."

When I disclosed the news to them up there they were all greatly astonished.

Zerah questioned me eagerly as to all I knew of John ben Zechariah, and of our meeting him on the hills near Gilboa, that day long ago, and as to what he and Jesus had said to one another.

And, though she was outwardly calm and sweet as usual, I thought I perceived in her an excitement which she found it difficult to hide. From the others she might, but she could not from me.

CHAPTER XXI

Of an Unexpected Visit

THAT year we had very heavy rains, and many cold winds from Hermon and the Lebanon, and my mother got some sickness that crippled her.

It was, I think, a kind of palsy, but it so bent and twisted her that she could do nothing for herself, much less for the household, and this caused her even more distress than the pain, though that was hard to bear.

Then indeed we had reason to bless Zerah. In the tenderest and most loving way she gave herself to the stricken mother—dressed her, fed her, cheered her with happy talk, always held out hopes of cure—did everything for her, and did it all as if it were a joy and a privilege.

For the rest of us it was a joy and a privilege to watch her, though we did all we could to help. For she was like an angel of light in the house. And in spite of the pain my mother suffered at times, Zerah succeeded in keeping her brave and cheerful.

I was as a rule very careful in the workshop, as Jesus, both by precept and example had taught me to be. But one day a nail, and a rusty one at

F

that, escaped me, and, lodging head between the boards and point upwards, in its own evil time it pierced my sandal and ran into my foot.

I suppose I did not give it proper care—I was extra busy at the time—for before long my foot swelled up and was very painful. I had to work as well as I could on one foot, with the other swathed in bandages. Fortunately Neri was getting on well and could do most of the small outside jobs. But I was much tied, and even when it did recover enough to let me set foot to earth, I had to go very cautiously or it broke out afresh and I had to begin the healing all over again.

I was working late one evening on a job that was urgently needed—for the work went slower on one leg than on two—when Jesus stepped quietly in through the doorway.

And so unexpected was he that I dropped my plane with a clatter and stood staring. For my thoughts had been full of him, and he seemed to me for a moment only an embodiment of them. I was not at all sure that he was real flesh and blood till he spoke to me. I had so often before imagined him there when he was not.

" It is myself, my Azor," he said gently. " Why are you so startled ? " and he came and kissed me on the cheek.

" Well, you see, I was thinking of you, and then, all of a sudden, there you were, and I thought you were in Kaphar-Nahum. I so often feel as if you were here when you are not."

" It is good to live in the hearts of one's friends," he said, with a smile, and asked, " What is wrong with your foot ? "

I told him, and had to acknowledge shame-facedly that it was all my own fault.

He shook his head in good-humoured reproval and said, " Nails in their right place are profitable, but one's foot is no place for them."

And then Zerah, hearing his voice, came running in from the house, her face radiant with welcome and the joy of seeing him again. She looked like falling on her knees before him, but his hands restrained her and he kissed her reverently and sweetly.

" You will stay with us ? " she asked eagerly.

" I will eat with you, but afterwards I must go up the hill. I had a great desire to see you all and the old home once more."

" We are glad," said Zerah. " We miss you greatly."

" It is good to be desired by one's friends. Azor took me for a spirit, but it is a spirit with a hungry body, for I have walked far," and Zerah laughed joyously at the hint and the opportunity of serving him, and ran in to tell the others and prepare the meal.

Zoe and the boys came hurrying to us and gave him warm welcome, and then Zoe went off to help Zerah, and Jesus took the boys one on each knee.

" But where is your mother ? " he asked.

I told him of her trouble, and he went in at

once, with a kicking boy on each shoulder, to see her.

He put the boys down by her bedside and was about to take her hands to greet her. But when he saw how warped and painful they were he stopped, and instead just patted them gently and stood looking wistfully down at her.

"You suffer, mother," he said softly. "And yet you are happy."

"They are all very good to me, Jesus, but I can do nothing for them in return," she sighed.

"They remember all you have done, Miriam. It is their turn now to serve you and I am sure they rejoice in their service."

"They are all good, but Zerah is an angel. I thank God many times in the day for sending her to us."

"He put the good seed into your own good heart and now you are gathering the harvest. It is well. We will all ask God for your relief," and he looked at her very wistfully again, for suffering, either in people or in animals, was always a sorrow to him.

Then he sat in the doorway again with the boys on his knees, and we talked till supper was ready.

"It is almost like the old times," Jesus said, as he sat there in the doorway, "and the rosemary is as fragrant as ever," but he looked round the old shop as though missing something, and I am sure it was Little Tobias.

"My mother often wishes she had her rosemary bushes with her at Kaphar-Nahum," he said.

" Take them back to her," I said. " They are hers."

" I've heard it said that it will not grow unless you steal it," he said with a smile.

" Then steal them."

" Stealing from you would not be stealing, my Azor," he laughed, " and one cannot steal from oneself. So we will let them stop where they are, and at times I will come and smell them for her."

Azor and Zadok sat very happily on his knees with his arms round them, but they were too young yet even to understand stories. They just sat and looked up into the loving, wistful face, and now and again stroked him with their small hands. And when the little hands went near his mouth he kissed them.

At supper he told us of the life at Kaphar-Nahum, and then spoke of his cousin John and of the good work he was doing by forcing people to think. And he said :

" I am going down there to see him——"

" And then ? " asked Zerah, in an eager whisper, so low that it was scarce more than a breath.

" Then—as God wills," he answered, in an equally low voice. And I think she understood, for her face was strained and uplifted. But his meaning was hidden from me at that time.

" I was going to ask you to company me on the road, Azor," he said. " For two together halve a journey if their hearts are knit. But with that foot it is out of the question. I must go alone."

So I paid dearly for my carelessness—more dearly than I then knew.

He asked as to this one and that one of the neighbours. He had heard, through Jotham and Miriam, of Judah's return home to old Amos. Jotham had been none too pleased at it at first. But as Judah had evidently learned his lesson, and had settled down to steady work, the past was forgiven and old Amos's heart was glad.

"And Dathan? How is he getting on?" Jesus asked, and that was a question we had all been dreading. His cousin Joses had gone with the rest to Kaphar-Nahum, and so he had not heard.

"He is doing very much better," I said at last.

"And little Ruth?"

And there we fell silent, for Dathan's poor little Ruth had fallen on sorrow.

Jesus looked round at us in surprise, and then said, "Nay then, tell me! What is the trouble?"

"She loved a man and trusted him overmuch," said Zerah pitifully.

"The poor child!" he said, very sadly. "Poor —little—maid! . . . And she always so sweet and modest! It was always a joy to meet her."

"Yes. Her only fault was in loving too much and trusting too much."

There was a flame in his eyes as he said sternly, "The sin was his, whoever he be. To him be the punishment! . . . But for her, poor child!" —and the stars in his eyes shone softly again—

" To one who loveth much, much shall be forgiven."

" She is dead, Jesus."

" It is well. She is with her Father. In His love she has peace and rest. Yes, it is better so."

But the thought of poor little Ruth's suffering and sorrow saddened him, and after a while he quietly bade us farewell and went alone up the hill, and we did not see him again.

CHAPTER XXII

Of a Greater Prophet still

It was not very long after that before the strange happenings began which altered all our lives, and—I can say it now, though at the time I could see no more than what passed before my eyes—which altered the whole life of the world.

They were so amazing, and—from an ordinary, matter-of-fact point of view—so entirely incomprehensible, that I doubt if I can make it, and all we felt about it, and its effect upon us, in any way clear to you.

You see, nothing like it, nothing we could ever possibly have dreamed of, in all its immensity and wonder, had ever befallen us. Though in that we were only like the rest of the world. We had, indeed, known what the rest of the world did not know, but that very knowledge was to some of us a hindrance rather than a help.

We had known and loved Jesus as a dear family friend, as a fellow-workman at the bench, as a thinker and dreamer on the hill-top. And now. . . .

No, it was not easy to readjust all one's thought of him in the past—happy beyond one's telling as all that was—and to fit this new, overwhelming conception of him into it.

Happenings so amazing, when one is quite close to them, are apt to be somewhat staggering and blinding.

I can think upon them all now very much more clearly than I could then. But my desire in this simple record is to show you, if I can, how it all appeared to us just at the time it was happening.

But from all this feeling of utter amazement I must leave out Zerah. It was to her—I was certain of it at the time, and she has since told me so herself—but the longed-for fulfilment of a mighty hope—a complete justification of her perfect trust—the crown of her self-sacrificing love.

The first we heard of it all was from Simon. He climbed the hill one night to tell us and was in a very curious state of mind—partly scornful, partly angry, and entirely amazed and confused. It was quite beyond him and it was that that upset him so.

Jesus, he told us, had gone down Jordan, with many others, to see John, and had not come back with the rest. Where he was they could not find out. He had disappeared and no man knew where he was.

We were very anxious about him. It was a wild and lonely country down that way. Anything might happen to him there.

And again, Zerah did not share our anxieties. She remained calm and undisturbed and went on with her work of looking after my mother and the rest of us, with as cheerful a grace as ever.

John and his mother, who were then with us, though they had never met him, were as excited as the rest of us.

"Let us go seek him, Azor!" said John eagerly.

"You will stop here, my son," said his mother very decisively. "And Azor has his work to do."

But I would have loved to go, work or no work, if my foot had permitted it.

Then, after what seemed a terribly long time of suspense and anxiety, Simon came panting up one night with the good news that Jesus was home again.

"But," he said—wagging his head in a way that very clearly expressed his own utter incomprehension and grave doubts as to Jesus's sanity— "He's come back different. He's not what he was before."

"How different, Simon?" asked Zerah quietly, in that beautiful rich voice of hers, and there was not a tremor in it, only eager longing.

"Well—he's setting up for a preacher and teacher himself now. And I can't see that there's much in it. . . . And he's different in himself. . . ."

"How different, Simon?" asked Zerah again.

"I don't know,"—Simon was never much of a thinker or speaker.—"Seems to me he's like what he was sometimes when he'd stopped out all

night up in the hills—only more so, if you can
understand what I mean, but now he's like that
all the time."

And Zerah, at all events, understood, I think.

" And are the people listening to him ? " she
asked, bending eagerly towards him.

" Oh, they're listening right enough. You
can't get into our courtyard for them—crowds
and crowds and crowds, all day long and never
had enough."

And Zerah sat back, her eyes and face glowing
softly with that inward illumination which I had
seen in her more than once before.

" You see," said Simon, scratching his head
bewilderedly, " they say he's doing things that
have never been seen before in this world——"

" What kind of things ? " asked Zerah, leaning
eagerly forward again.

" Well "—he said, a trifle shamefacedly, as
though he feared how we might receive it—" they
do say he's set some people free from demons
that have possessed them. And they say he's
cured some people of their sicknesses, though the
physicians hadn't been able to. I've not seen
anything of all that myself, but everyone's talking
about it, so there must be something in it. And
I did see Joanan ben Josech last night and he
seemed quite all right. And if anyone ever was
possessed of a devil it was Joanan. And there is
old Jabez the leper. Everyone knows him well,
his skin's as wholesome as mine now. And it was
our Jesus did it—just with a word and a touch.

So everyone's carrying their sick folk up to our house——"

"And he heals them ? " said Zerah.

"Yes, so they say.   But it's all beyond me and I don't know what to make of it."

We none of us knew what to make of it—except Zerah, who, as I now know, understood very much more than most.

The next news we had was that Jesus had left home and was going about the country teaching and preaching, and curing many sick folk, with some of the lake-men, who had given up their work to be with him ; and great crowds were meeting him everywhere and were following him.

It made me restless to go and seek him again. I would have loved to see and hear him and be with him once more.   It was all very astounding and quite beyond me.   But when Simon told us that he told the people many stories and at times made them laugh, I could just imagine him doing it, and I knew those stories of his would never be forgotten.

Many times young John proposed that we two should go and hear him.   But his mother, eager as she was herself to see Jesus, deemed him too young for such a journey, and Zoe and my mother were against my attempting it.

Zerah said quietly : "Wait, Azor.   He will certainly come back here in time," and her face was all alight those days with the certainty she felt of seeing him again before long.

CHAPTER XXIII

OF HIS COMING TO HIS OWN

IT seemed to us a very long time, and it was;
but at last we heard that he was coming to
Nazaret, and we were all agog with impatience
till we should see him.

We heard and saw, by the crowds below, when
he arrived, and young John and I went hurrying
down the path so fast that we kept falling over
our feet, for one of mine was not much good
and John's went faster than his body.

But, before we got to the bottom, Jesus was
beginning to climb to meet us, and at sight of
our stumbling haste his wonderful eyes lighted up
with a welcoming smile and his face was joyous.

It was partly the roughness of the path and our
eagerness, and partly—yea, I am sure mostly—
something new in himself that almost blinded me
and took my breath—but whatever it was, as we
met him we both found ourselves on our knees,
and gazing up at him in wonder.

With a hand to each of us he lifted us to our
feet and kissed us both on the cheek.

"It is a joy to see you again, my Azor," he
said, and his voice was fuller and richer and
sweeter than ever. "And who is this?"

" It is John, who lives with his mother in our old house. They are from Jerusalem. He has been aching to meet you. So has his mother. And so have we all. See—they come—all of them ! " for Zerah and Zoe, and John's mother, and Azor and Zadok were hurrying down the path above us to give him welcome.

That first meeting of Jesus and Zerah, after all that time, I never shall forget.

He looked more like my idea of what a mighty leader of men should be than ever before. And she was radiant and passing good to look upon. I had never seen her so supremely beautiful. That wonder, as of a holy inward light, seemed to fill her and overflow from her, as the sun shines through the morning mist.

I watched them, breathless.

His all - comprehending eyes were full of a feeling far beyond my understanding as they dwelt lovingly upon her. Hers, as they met his, were brave and trustful, and deep and luminous with love—great stars in the Pools of Heshbon.

" God's sweet grace be yours for ever, Zerah ! " he said deeply, and kissed her as he used to kiss his mother.

" Amen ! " she said, softly and sweetly—as she did that first day they ever met.

Then he greeted the others, and filled Zoe's heart to the brim with his cordial praise of her sons.

" And you live at Jerusalem ? " he said to John's mother.

" When we have to, Master," she said, somewhat overcome, I think, by his dignified presence. " But we live better here. They need you badly down there though."

" Everywhere the need cries aloud," he said gravely.

Then he turned to me, " And how is Miriam—your mother, Azor ?   Is she still prisoner ? "

" She is waiting for you in the house, Jesus. Her trouble still holds her, but she has been longing to see you again."   And he quickened his pace up the hill-path which his feet knew so well.

We passed through the workshop and into the living-room, which had been home to him for so many happy years.

My mother was lying on her bed—her thin face and bright eyes straining for the sight of him.

He went up to her and took her poor twisted hands in both of his, and looked down at her with two heavens of compassion brimming his eyes.

" In the name of our Father ! " he said gently.

And as we stood and watched amazed, those poor crooked hands straightened themselves grate-fully in his. The shaking arms ceased their troublous moving and clung to him with new life. Her thin, worn face glowed with a mighty hope. And presently, her hands still in his, she rose to her feet as if he had lifted her. And when he let go her hands she walked—she who had not set foot to the ground for years.

She fell on her knees, sobbing for joy, and her

joy overcame even her wonder at the marvel of it. For the time being she could think of nothing but the fact that whereas she was helpless now she could walk. The wonder of it remained with her all her life.

She fell on her knees and clutched his robe and brokenly sobbed her gratitude. He raised her again with a glad face and said gently, " Give thanks to Him, Miriam, and of your goodness get me something to eat, for I am hungry," and she set rejoicingly to provide for him.

The rest of us were too amazed to speak. But Zerah, with a joyous face, said quietly, " I hoped you would," and he smiled very tenderly at her.

And as my mother got ready our meal, with the glad energy of her years of enforced rest, she told him of all that Zerah had been to her and to all of us, and could not find words for it all.

We sat in the sunset that night as we used to do, and he told us of his journeyings, and spoke hopefully of the eagerness of many of the people to hear his message.—And sadly of some who would not.

Before he came, when we were hoping he might sometime come, we had been full of questions we wanted to ask him. Now that he was sitting in our midst, so great upon us was the awe and wonder of that most amazing thing that he had done for us, that our tongues were tied, and we could only sit and listen.

Zerah alone was just herself ; uplifted indeed,

but calm and rational, and she asked him many things we longed to know.

I listened eagerly to all he said, but, I suppose because my mind was in such a turmoil, I remember only the general sense of it. And, besides, there was much that I could not then comprehend.

And, you must remember, this marvellous new power of his was very upsetting to me who had seen him sweating with saw and hammer at that bench just behind him. That very hammer lying on the bench was the one his hands had used. And now I had seen those same hands give new life to a shrunken body. It is no wonder it took me, and the rest, some time to fit this new Jesus into the new place he must occupy in our hearts and lives.

I gathered, from the quiet talk between him and Zerah, that the call to some great work for God had been growing and growing in him, always growing stronger and stronger, while he lived here — that the preaching of his cousin John, and his vehement assertions that the Kingdom was close at hand—and chiefly something that took place when he met John on the banks of Jordan and was baptized by him there —had made it a certainty to him.

He had felt wondrous new power given to him, and now, heart and soul and body, he was to devote himself to the work.

And, from the way they spoke together, I knew that it had been discussed by them before, and that there was perfect understanding between them.

In a pause in their talk he picked up one of my yokes that was standing there, and ran his fingers carefully over it, just as he used to do. Then he nodded smilingly to me and said :

" Good work, Azor ! You keep them up to our standard."

" I do them, and all else, as I think you would wish them done."

" It is well," he said gently. " The poor dumb brothers ! Easy yoke makes burden light. I have been devising a happier pack-saddle for the camels. But they are not very grateful as yet, or they don't know how to show it."

CHAPTER XXIV

Of the Return of Arni

Jesus slept in his own old room that night, Zerah joyously going in with my mother.

Very early in the morning three of his followers came seeking him. They were named Simon and James and John, and all three, before they gave up their work to follow him, had been fishermen on the Lake.

But he told them he would spend that day up aloft and would join them in the village that night or the following day, and they went down again.

"You and I are for the hills to-day, my Azor," he said joyously. "For to-day we will be boys again. We have hills not far away at Kaphar-Nahum, but my heart turns oftener to the hills of Nazaret. The days here were very happy days."

"May I come too?" asked young John eagerly.

"Can you walk far and keep up with us?"

"I'm sure I can, with you, Master. Azor can tell you. I'm a good walker, and I can swim too."

"You shall come."

And Zerah, when she heard, begged to go too,

and he would not say her nay, for he understood all that was in her.

" It will not be too much for you ? " he asked.

" Not with you," she answered, and so it was agreed.

So, after eating, we four set out, and Jesus led us by the hill-paths, and across the plain and the stream, to that hill where once, long before, we two had met his cousin John, and they had sat and talked of things beyond me.

It was no small walk, but to my great amazement my foot never troubled me all the way. In fact I had never once thought of it.

It was only when we flung ourselves down that the surprise of it came upon me.

" My foot is healed," I said, looking up at him in wonder, and, I think, after what he had done for my mother, in some dim way ascribing it to him.

He just smiled at me and said gently, " Try to keep all the nails in their proper place in future, Azor."

And, however it was, my foot troubled me no more.

We had brought cakes and fruit with us, and we lay long on the hill-top, looking across at Tabor and Gilboa, and he spoke quietly, but with feeling so deep and intense that it awed me again, of his mission and the way people were receiving it.

I did not as yet understand very much of what it all meant, though I think Zerah did.

He jumped up suddenly and stood gazing earnestly out towards the village that lay below us. From the gateway had issued a small company carrying a bier, and was coming towards the hill.

It was the meagreness of the following which appealed to him, I think. For it consisted of one solitary woman, and that was just the kind of thing that would touch his heart.

"Let us go down," he said, and we followed him. And as the scanty procession drew near, he said, very tenderly, "A widow . . . and poor, since there are none with her. And probably her only son. . . . Poor Mother!"

When the bearers met us he made a sign to them to stop. The forlorn little mother stood and stared at us in wonder and reproach. Her face was very sad and worn and her eyes were red with weeping.

Jesus regarded her steadfastly for a moment. Then he bade the bearers set down the bier, and they wonderingly did so.

He stood looking down at the dead man who lay on it wrapped in his cerements. Then he leaned over him and said quietly, "Arni— Koum!"

And slowly—slowly and heavily—the dead man opened his eyes and lay looking up into his face— full of tenderest love and pity.

Then he sat up, struggling to free his arms from the folds of the wrapper, and tore the linen bandages off his face. His face was lean and shrunken, and out of their deep hollows his eyes stared mistily with dawning recognition.

" Jesus ! " he gasped.

And Jesus took him by the hand and lifted him off the bier.

" Little Mother," he said joyously, " your Father gives him back to you for happier times. Serve ye Him all your days ! "

The amazed little woman fell on her son's breast, weeping as though her mind had gone. And then she slipped down to the ground, and knelt and kissed the folds of Jesus's robe.

" To God your thanks, Mother ! " he said softly, and lifted her up. " See now—Arni is hungry. Take him home and give him to eat."

Arni's face—the wonder, the awe, and very much more, that no man, I think, could understand—remains stamped upon my memory. I can see it now. I wondered often if he ever again looked quite as other men. For he had been dead—and was alive again.

He fell on his knees before Jesus, and knelt there, gazing up into his face. And Jesus put his hands on his head and blessed him, and then lifted him up and kissed him, and said, " Think of me, Arni ! Do as you know I would have you do. Tend your mother, and be as a light to your neighbours. And may the blessing of God rest upon you ! "

Then he turned and led us quickly away up the hill. For the bearers, when they saw the dead sit up, had fled to the village, and now the whole population came pouring out of the gate and was running towards us.

Zerah's face, as we went, was full of rapture and streaming with tears—a bright sun shining through joyous rain. Young John's eyes were nearly falling out, and his face was blank with awe and amazement. For myself, I went blindly— my feet stumbling along of their own accord, my mind groping helplessly for something to hold on to.

For I had, with my own two eyes, seen a dead man, and one whom I had known and loved, raised to life again—an incredible thing!—an impossible thing! . . . But I had *seen* it, and it was!

And the doer of this incredible and impossible thing strode lightly on in front there—the dearest and closest friend I had ever had—my fellow-workman at our own carpenter's bench— a man like myself. . . .

But there I brought up sharply, as a man in the dark bumps up against a wall, and, dazed, stands and gropes to discover where he is.

A man—like—myself! . . . But a man like myself could not do things like that!

Then this, my friend, with whom I had played, and swam, and walked, and talked, and worked, was not simply a man like myself!

What then? And—who? And how? . . . I was a man against a wall in the dark—stunned and dazed, and not knowing where I was or which way to turn!

Looking back I saw all the people of the village gathered round Arni and his mother, all talking excitedly and staring after us as we climbed the hill.

We went in silence for a very long time—down the other slope, across the plain and the stream, and began the opposite ascent.

Then Jesus, looking back, caught sight of Zerah's face, and motioned to us to sit and rest.

My heart and my mind—yea, and my very soul —were in a turmoil of perplexity. I was bursting to know—to know—as I now know—what no mortal man could tell me, for the full of it was beyond the mind of mortal man to grasp. For the soul can believe and trust where the heart accepts in faith, but the mind has little help to give in such a matter, and sometimes provides but stumbling-blocks.

I sat gazing at him dumbly—as little Tobias used to do—worshipfully, lovingly, but without understanding, except that he was altogether good and lovable, and very wonderful, and of a higher order than myself.

The others, I know, must have been feeling much as I did. John sat gazing at him with eyes which looked as if they would never again lose their amazement.

Zerah's shining eyes were fixed on him too, but in them were unspeakable love, perfect trust, and a rapt touch of exultant understanding, as of one whose blind faith has been suddenly blessed with sight.

Jesus sat gazing thoughtfully out over the plain, where a shepherd was collecting his flock for the homeward trail. I knew that deep intent look of his so well; and when it was on him I had never ventured to disturb him. But that which was in me was beyond my power to contain.

"Who then ? . . . What . . . ?" jerked out through my dry lips.

He turned and looked lovingly at me, and said, "It is my Father's work, Azor. I but do His will—His good will to men——"

"Your. . . ."

His father ? . . . Joseph, the carpenter ? . . . But . . . but . . .

And then the scales fell from my startled eyes and I saw what he meant . . . and the immensity of it—the overwhelming wonder and magnitude of it.

"You . . . mean . . . *God* ?" I whispered.

"Is He not my Father and your Father ? . . . The Father of us all ? . . . He has sent me to call His children back to Him. They have strayed like sheep, but He wants them, every one."

The sheep on the plain below were following the shepherd to the ford in a long straggling line. The still air was full of their bleatings as the lambs sought their dams.

"Are you . . . Are you . . . the Deliverer then ?" I whispered, awestricken.

"By the good will of my Father," he said quietly.

"And you will drive out the Romans and give

us our right place in the world," said John, bursting through the amazement which had held him.

Jesus was silent for a time, and the far-away look in his eyes seemed to go away past us, right out over the whole world.

Then he said gently, "There are greater Kingdoms than Rome, John, and greater things than driving the Romans into the sea. . . . The will of my Father is for the greatest things of all."

"Let me go with you to help!" I said eagerly.

"And I!" said Zerah, in her rich fluty voice, which trembled with the flood of her feelings.

"And I!" piped John, starting up from the ground.

But Jesus shook his head and said, gently but very decisively, "No . . . Zerah, Azor, your work lies to your hand in the home and beyond it. . . . What would become of the home, Azor, if you left it to follow me?"

And I was silent, for I knew the home would starve, since there was none but me to feed it.

"In it," he said, "you can both follow me as truly as if you trod the path I tread. . . . Little John, stay now with your mother and do her bidding! . . . Sometime, perhaps. . . . But in all things, all of you, strive to think of your fellows as The Father thinks—your Father and my Father. And do to them as He would have you do. . . ." And after a moment's thought, he said, "If that is beyond you as yet—you know me and my way of thinking—think of them in the

way you know I would think of them, and do to
them as you know I would do. For in this I
and my Father are one. . . . Come, let us be
going ! " and we followed him up the hill, in
silence and overfull of our thoughts.

CHAPTER XXV

Of his Rejection by his Own

THE next day was the Sabbath, and we all—
and my mother—went down with him to the
synagogue. It was the first time in three years
that she had been able to go, and the neighbours
were amazed at the sight of her.

I shrink from the recollection of that day, for
it shows our people of Nazaret at their worst.

There was quite a crowd in the village, for they
had already got word of the raising of Arni from
the dead, and all were eager to see the man who
could do such wonders.

His followers were there waiting for him, and
they made a way for us into the synagogue.
The roll was handed to him and he read from the
Prophet. And he read—not as they were in the
habit too often of hearing, in a dull monotonous
drone—but clearly and weightily, in that full
rich voice which gave a new authority to the
words and played upon one's heart and made every
word sink into it.

This is what he read. I have never forgotten
it, because, in the light of my new perception of

him, it seemed to me to speak so exactly about himself.

> "The Spirit of the Lord is upon me, for He has consecrated me to preach the good news to the poor,
> He has sent me to proclaim release for captives, and recovery of sight to the blind, to set free the oppressed, to proclaim the Lord's year of favour."

Then he handed the roll back and sat down, and they all waited eagerly for him to speak.

And when he did speak they were astounded. For he said, so that every man heard it :

"To-day . . . this scripture is fulfilled in your hearing."

They grasped his meaning, and a gust of resentful whispering ran through them.

"What does he mean ? " I heard. " Isn't he the carpenter ? " . . . " Haven't we known him all his life, and all his folk ? " . . . "The spirit of the Lord upon *him !* Well, what next ? " . . . " Of all the impudence ! " . . . " But what about Arni ? " . . " And Miriam ? " . . . " All the same. . . ."—and much more of the like.

"Quite so ! " he said quietly. " A prophet receives no honour in his own country—nor ever did," and, grieved at their perversity, he added, " It always has been so. There were many widows in Israel at the time of the great famine, but Elijah was sent, not to one of them, but to— a widow in Sidon. And there were many lepers in Israel in the time of Elisha, yet none of them was cleansed, but instead—Naaman the Syrian."

That bit deep and made them furious. They all sprang up and foamed and howled at him and would have clutched and struck him. I thrust through them to get to my women-folk on the other side.

But Zerah was up and trying to make her way to him. "Foolish! Foolish and wicked!" she cried. "Are you all blind? Can you not see what he is?"—But, as the others seemed in no danger, I climbed the barrier and helped to clear her way by digging my elbows into any who hindered her, and I did it with gusto.

But before we could get anywhere near him, his followers had closed round him, and then— I thought suddenly of the path cleared through the Red Sea when Moses lifted his rod. For Jesus just looked at them with those great calm compelling eyes of his, and they wavered and broke before him, and he and his people passed out unharmed. When we saw he was safe we went back to my mother and Zoe and the others, and by the time we were able to get into the street he had disappeared.

We went up home sadly, for we knew how this rebuff could not but pain him, and could we have had our way we would have removed every obstacle from his path.

After that, for a long time, we got little word of him, and Simon who was our chief news-bringer was not a very satisfactory reporter. He picked up all the tittle-tattle of the Lake towns, but only the exciting things appealed to him and so got through to us.

We heard of Jesus going into Judea and to Jerusalem, and of vast multitudes following him everywhere, even into the deserts, to listen to his teaching. We heard of some of the wonders he did—lepers cleansed, blind given their sight, many sick cured, several more dead folk restored to life, great crowds numbering thousands fed in some mysterious way with nothing but a handful of loaves.

We heard that his fame was become so great by reason of these things, and by his wonderful teaching, so unlike any that had ever been heard before, that the great mass of the people were convinced that he was the Promised Deliverer and wanted to proclaim him King. And we heard too, and could well understand, that the rulers were very bitter against him. For the things he taught were so different from what they taught that there was not room in the world for both them and him.

Up in our quiet home on the hillside we followed his doings with hearts abrim, and wondered what the end of it all would be. But at times we got no news of him for weeks on end. All Simon could tell us was that he was away and nobody knew where.

Zerah treasured every scrap of news Simon brought us, but suffered much from the longing she had to see and hear him herself again.

When we heard of the imprisonment of John
the Baptizer by King Herod, she was filled with
fears for Jesus. Prophets, she said, generally paid
with their lives, and it would be so with him.

And when later on the word came of John's
beheading in the Castle of Machaerus, her sweet
high spirit suffered a heavy blow. She was, I
could see, full of forebodings, though she carried
herself very bravely.

Zerah craved above all things to see Jesus once
more, and the craving grew so fierce in her that
we feared it would consume her strength entirely.

And so, for her sake, it was settled that she and
I and young John—who flatly refused to be left
behind—should visit Kaphar-Nahum as soon as
we heard that Jesus in his journeyings was to be
there again.

Simon at last brought us word that he was there
and would be there for yet another day or two.

" Resting ? " asked Zerah hopefully.

" Resting ! He takes no rest. The folk give
him no chance—except when he goes away by
himself into the hills now and again. They run
after him in thousands and are always wanting
more. We don't know how he stands it. He
must be made of iron. And he looks it. He
never tires. He's like an eagle—only he cures,
not kills."

So we made our arrangements at once. Simon
was starting at dawn with his asses and would
give Zerah, at all events, a lift. John and I
would have to walk.

We were to be at Peleg's house before daybreak. So my mother and Zerah and Zoe set to work at once baking cakes for our journey.

We were up and dressed in the dark. John, who said he had not dared to close his eyes lest he should be late, came along from the other house with his mother, and we bade them all farewell and set off.

And then, as we stumbled down the rough hill-path, a strange thing happened. And to this day I have never ceased to be sorry for it. For it deprived me of what I had greatly desired, and the opportunity was never vouchsafed me again.

Most people have seen at some time or other a tree that has fallen through old age or been blown down in a storm. And we have all of us seen here and there a house or a tower that has sunk into ruin. But it is not given to many to see the tree as it falls or the house as it sinks.

We were passing Naggai's house at the foot of the hill. We could not indeed see much, for it was still dark, but, helped by our ears, we could perceive what happened even if we could not actually see it.

At the very moment of our passing there came a strange muffled rush and roar—a sound like ' r-r-r-r-ruff '—then a moment's startling silence, and then a heavy creaking and falling—and groans and cries.

I scrambled over the wall—and in doing it, thought of that day long ago when Jesus and I went over it to the rescue of Tobias.

I knew at once what must have happened, for, if I had warned Naggai once about that sagging south wall of his house, I had warned him a dozen times. He was always going to have it seen to but never did. And now it had gone, before our very eyes, as you might say; and, deprived of its help, the roof had sunk down upon those within.

My duty was there to my hand. " Run on you two and tell the nearest neighbours. Tell them to bring spades. . . . And then go you on with Simon. You can do nothing here. I will follow you as soon as I can."

They sped away and I set to work as well as I could, groping in the dark amid that dreadful confusion and the cries and groans of the buried ones, for what of life I might find.

That they were not all killed outright was evident, but it was desperately difficult to do anything useful in that half-darkness. I did what I could, and I knew that the neighbours and daybreak could not be far away.

" Where are you—Naggai ?—Elizabeth ?— Damaris ? "—his wife and daughter, the one whom Tobias used to waken with his barking. Nachor had long since gone away—to sea, which I always thought was the best place for him.

Smothered cries alone answered me, for the heavy roof, with its floor of trampled earth, had sunk in on them, and but for its big cross-beams would have stifled them at once.

I began hauling blindly at anything my groping

hands could clutch, and then I saw the unwisdom of zeal without knowledge, for I might but loosen any protection the fallen beams were affording them and so but add to their peril.

The darkness thinned suddenly and I heard the neighbours panting up the path, and presently there were a dozen of them there and we could see what we were about.

It was all a terrible mess and not easy to know where to begin. While the others delved with hands and spades I ran up the hill for a couple of saws, to the vast astonishment of my Mother and Zoe who supposed me on the way to Kaphar-Nahum.

It took some hours' hard work and the sawing through of a couple of big beams before we could drag them out one by one—all more or less bruised and still terribly frightened.

It was only the slow sinking of the roof, with the beams at an angle, that saved their lives.

Little Damaris, white and shaking still, I took up to our house, and my mother and Zoe tended her. Naggai and Elizabeth were taken in by neighbours below.

But the strain of the work, and still more the desperate fear all the time that after all we might be too late, had exhausted me completely. When at last we recovered them I felt as if I had been in a battle and had been worsted. Zerah and John and Simon would be halfway to Kaphar-Nahum, and much as I longed to be with them I had to give it up. I lay flat most of that day, finding myself again, and was no good for anything.

Zerah and John came back with Simon on the third day, very full of all they had seen and heard. And Zerah was very much happier in her mind thereafter, though I know she always went in fear that King Herod would sooner or later take Jesus and kill him, as he had done his cousin John.

She and young John told us about it all between them, first one then the other breaking in as new bits of their great experience came back to them.

They had found nearly all the town gone out to the slope of a hill some distance away, and had followed them there.

" And he was sitting there on a lump of rock, leaning forward with his elbow on his knee, talking to them just like a big elder brother to a lot of children—not at all as the priests talk to them," said Zerah. " And they listened just like children, with wide eyes and open mouths, and now and again laughing out at the way he put things. Oh, it was wonderful ! . . . wonderful ! " she said, with shining face and eyes. " We were right on the outside of the crowd but we could hear every word."

" And what was he talking about ? " asked John's mother, whose interest in Jesus was growing all the time.

" Ah, if I could only tell you it all ! " said Zerah, raising her clasped hands. " It was ' Blessed ! . . . blessed ! . . . blessed ! . . .' Oh, it was wonderful ! " and she pressed her palms over her eyes as if to bring it all back to her mind, all she had seen and heard that day.

" And," she said, " you see, it was all so strange and new. For he said those were blessed whom the world does not consider so—the poor—the hungry—those who weep—those whom men hate and cast out."

" Strange teaching, indeed ! " said John's mother, thoughtfully.

" . . . And those who hunger and thirst——" broke in John, as if that had struck him most.

" —after right," added Zerah.

" —And the merciful and peacemakers, and ever so many more," said John. " I could not understand it all, but it did me good to listen to it. And he told us some stories——"

" He was sure to do that," I said.

" And he made them laugh about a man with a plank in his eye trying to take a splinter out of his brother's eye."

" And then his ' Woe's ' ! " said Zerah—" Woe to the rich—the well-fed—those whom men speak well of—those who laugh now."

" And if a man hits you on the cheek you should ask him to hit the other cheek as well," said John, enjoying our surprise. " And if he takes your coat you should give him your shirt too ! "

" And—love your enemies !—and judge nobody ! " said Zerah.

" Very strange teaching ! " said my mother. " It is just what he would do himself but it will

not be easy for the rest of us. . . . Did you see
Mary, Zerah ?—and what is she feeling about it
all ? "

" She fears, I think, that it will get him into
trouble—especially since they did his cousin John
to death. Her face is very anxious and her eyes
are full of forebodings."

" Ay," said my mother. " She will suffer sorely
if any ill befalls him. He is the apple of her eye,
but I doubt if she has ever quite understood him."

" He is beyond any of our understanding—or
of any man's," I said. " Did you speak with
him, Zerah ? "

" I did," she said, her face radiant, her eyes very
bright. " Amid all that crowd his eyes found me.
It was wonderful! I was gazing hungrily at
him, and his eyes came slowly round, searching,
searching, as though he knew I was there. And
then they lighted on mine, though we were
almost the furthest out, and it was as though a
flash of lightning struck me and shook my soul.
. . . But," she added, dreamily, joyously, " it
was the lightning of his great love and it filled me
with unspeakable joy. . . . And, when he had
bidden them all go home, he came to us and
spoke to us. . . ." She fell silent, savouring
again, I think, what he had said to her. But all
she told us was—" And he bade us all be of good
cheer and not let our hearts be troubled."

And presently she said, " He asked for you at
once, Azor." I nodded, for I was sure he would
wonder at my not being there. " And when I

told him how eager you had been to come, and about Naggai's house falling down, he said, ' Azor did right to stop and help them. He knew I would have done that. It is better to do even than to listen '."

" He's a very wonderful man," said John's mother.

" How very wonderful we none of us really know," said Zerah thoughtfully.

CHAPTER XXVI

Of our Journey through the Valley of Shadows

I DRAW near the end. And I shrink from the telling of it, though I know now that the wonder and the glory of it all exceed, beyond the comprehension of man, what to us at the time was all heart-breaking sorrow.

Not one of us up there in our house on the hillside but believed absolutely that Jesus, the dearest friend we had ever had, was the Chosen One of God—the Promised Deliverer, the long-looked-for Messiah—the One who should establish God's Kingdom on earth. As to exactly what that Kingdom was we were not very clear. Nor as to how the friend, who had played and worked and lived with us as a boy and as a man, who had grown up amongst us in the closest relationship, should have become what he was.

But that he was more than man our hearts told us beyond the possibility of doubt.

We were filled with awe when we acknowledged to ourselves what we believed him to be. But the beauty and joy and wonder of the love he had given us were greater even than the awe which hardly dared to whisper its belief.

For months at a time we heard little of him, save that at times no one seemed to know where he was, and then again we would hear of him journeying slowly through distant parts of the country, up in the Lebanon, round Tyre and Sidon, and in many out-of-the-way villages and places.

And everywhere the people, when he spoke to them, listened to him gladly and followed him in crowds—everywhere . . . except in his own village of Nazaret; where he came no more. They had rejected him and he had much to do.

We hoped always that he would come again, but we did not then know how short his time was.

John and his mother were in Jerusalem. They generally came to us soon after the Passover.

My mother was well and active, rejoicing once more in all her household duties. Zoe had her hands full with the boys, active little fellows, always in mischief. I looked forward to the time when they would be to me what John had been, what I had been to Jesus. What times we would have in the workshop! What rambles over the hills and swims in the pool!

Zerah was quite beyond my understanding in these days. My experience of women, outside my own circle, was very small. I could only reason about Zerah on the lines I knew, and she was altogether beyond them.

She was gracious and sweet and good to us all, as she always had been; but I could not help feeling at times that, though in the body she was with us, in the spirit she was away with Jesus in his wanderings—following him everywhere, listening to him, watching him hungrily, as she had done that day on the hill at Kaphar-Nahum—perhaps communing with him in the spirit.

For at times, as we all sat together of an evening, her spindle would slowly cease its spinning, and she would sit in deep thought, with her eyes on the distant hills, till something called her back to us.

And at times, and more often as the months drew on, she would go off quietly by herself up the hill. And, from the calm in her eyes and the sweet high look on her face when she came back, I think she spent much of the time up there in prayer.

Simon brought us such news as he heard, but it was always much the same—ceaseless journeyings, teaching that drew crowds, many wonders of healing and help, ever-growing belief among the people that the time of deliverance had come at last.

Then, one night he came up with the word that Jesus was on his way to Jerusalem for the Passover.

The next morning Zerah came to me while I was at work and said, quietly, but in a way that showed me her mind was quite made up, " Azor, my brother, I want you to take me to Jerusalem for the Passover."

And I straightened up from my work and stared at her.

" If you won't take me I must go alone, but it would be more seemly——"

" But wherefore, Zerah ? I don't understand."

" Do you not see ? " she said, with deepest earnestness. " He is going there to bring matters to a head. . . . There he will win all, or . . . or . . ."

" Or lose all," I said, with a catch in my breath at thought of what his going might mean—to himself—to all of us.

" He may lose his life, for he told me that might be. But—lose all ! . . ." she said, with that far-away look in her shining eyes. " He can never lose what he has done . . . or what he is——"

" He may lose his life," I said again, and my heart sank low.

" He who loses his life shall save it—he said so himself. . . . The fear of losing his life is the last thing that will stop him. He counts it as nothing compared with that which he has to do. It is we who will suffer. . . . Will you take me, Azor ? . . . If he should fall on trouble perhaps I might be able to minister to him in some way," and she looked at me so piteously that I said :

" Yes, we will go," and she set about our preparations at once.

From that moment she was as one in whom a flaming white fire of devotion to an idea overpowers every other thought. And so she was throughout. She was very wonderful.

Zoe and my mother said nothing against our going. I think it likely that Zerah had already discussed it with them.

Two days before the usual time for the Passover company to start, she came to me and said, " Azor, my brother, can we go before the others ? " and in answer to my look of surprise, for it was customary all to travel together, she said, very earnestly, " You see, he may choose to get there before the crowds and possibly we might get speaking with him again. Oh, if you knew how my heart craves the sight of him ! . . . And—truly, I could not bear to journey with so many of those who treated him so despitefully. Do let us go on ahead of them, Azor ! "

And, understanding somewhat of all that was in her, I agreed, and we set off very early in the morning of the next day.

It was a wonderful Spring. Everything, even the bare rounded summits of the hills, seemed bursting with the very joy of living. The Great Plain, as we struck across it and forded the river to join the South Road, was knee-deep in flowers. When the West wind swept in up the river valley, it was like a mighty carpet being shaken by giant hands—such a carpet as they weave out there in the desert towns, the colours all mixed, yet blending all into a most wonderful whole. And the air was like honey in the comb.

But we had both made the journey many times before, I more often than she ; and our hearts went so much faster than our feet, and were so charged with anxious thought, that we gave but little heed to the things about us.

Life or Death awaited us at Jerusalem. Our only desire was to get there as quickly as possible.

CHAPTER XXVII

Of the Tumultuous City

We slept that first night at the little khan in Ginæa, and the next day crossed the hills into Samaria. The New City, with its rows of great white columns, we passed by, and walked along the river-side up the valley to Shechem, or Sychar as its own people call it.

It is a very fertile and beautiful land along that valley, and whenever I passed through it I always thought that if I had to live in Samaria it was that Vale of Shechem I would choose.

Ebal, with its sunny slopes covered with vines and olives and pomegranates, was on our left hand, and on the right, Gerizim, dark and shadowy, with gaping black mouths along its base which made one think of tombs and robbers and evil spirits.

We slept at a little inn I knew of at Sychar, and were afoot again with the dawn. Just outside the town we stopped at Jacob's Well to fill our water-bottles, for its water is the coolest and sweetest you can find in all that country.

But the taste of it was somewhat spoiled for us that day by the sight of a great wooden cross on a mound by the side of the road, and on it the pitiful remains of what had been a man. There was not very much of him left beyond his bones, for the winds and the weather and the birds had had their way with him.

But the titulus above his head was still clear for all who passed to read—

BARGAS—THIEF AND MURDERER

and I suppose he was left hanging there as a warning to his fellows. His evil deeds lived after him.

Zerah's sweet face puckered distastefully at sight of him, and we filled our bottles quickly and were about to hurry on, when a voice pealed out above our heads and we stopped and looked up and round in great surprise, for we were the first on the road and there was no one to be seen.

"Ho—Rebek-kah! Where is Isaac to-day?" cried the voice, clear and strong on the still morning air.

And the oddness of the two names together in that place made us wonder if it could be haunted by the spirits of the past.

But when again we heard above us, in a sweet girlish voice—"He got a thorn in his foot and cannot walk"—we knew that it was not spirits speaking.

"I will come to-night," said the boy's voice.

"I shall be glad," said the girl.

And then we discovered, away up on the side of Gerizim, bathed now in the clear early sunshine, a white flock of sheep and a boy standing like a little pillar among them. And on the far-away sunny slope of Ebal was a dark flock of goats, with a girl in a yellow robe behind them. And I thought of Zerah and Zoe that first day I ever set eyes on them, and the Song of Songs—" Dark streams your hair like goats adown the slopes of Gilead. . . . Your teeth like shorn ewes paired together in rows."

The thought of the boy and girl and their rustic love sent us on our way more happily, but Zerah hurried past Bargas with pinched face and her head turned the other way.

" Perhaps he deserved it," she said, " but men are very cruel."

" If he was a thief and a murderer, he deserved it."

" I don't know. . . . There might be better ways, even with thieves and murderers," she said thoughtfully, and we pressed on.

That night we slept at Beth-El, and all the way along, every hill-path now had its string of travellers making for the highway — like little streams that trickle downwards to the river.

The Great Road was already black with people all hurrying to Jerusalem. It seemed to me more crowded than I had ever seen it before, and it made me think of a great swarm of locusts, pressing ever on and on. For there was in their bearing an unusual intentness and eagerness, as of men who went in expectation of something out of the common.

And so we came into Jerusalem by the Damascus Gate, in the afternoon of the fourth day, and were well pleased to have got to the end of our journey.

The City seemed to us already overflowing with people, and we were thankful that we had not to seek a lodging but could go as usual straight to the house of John's mother, Mary, which had always been open to us for the Passover.

Her house was on Mount Zion, not far from that of the High Priest, and we had no little difficulty in making our way there. It was the most toilsome and trying part of our journey. And when at last we reached the house, hot and dusty with the road, and still more weary with pushing through the crowds, it was only to learn that, for the first time, Mary could not take us in.

We saw her, but only for a moment. She was in a state of great excitement and exaltation, quite unlike her usual placid self.

" I am sorry, sorry," she said, " but The Teacher himself is coming to eat the Passover here. What can I do ? What can I do ? " and then, casting about in her mind, she said, " See now, at Bethany is my Sister Rachel. Tell her I sent you and she will find you room, I am sure. . . . Truly, I am sorry, children, but you see how I am placed. The Teacher himself. . . ."

" Where is Jesus, Mary ? " asked Zerah, eagerly.

" We do not know, child. He goes out of the City most nights, with his followers. And maybe he is wise. There is great excitement among the people. You can see it for yourselves—and Annas and Caiaphas are very wroth about it. But he will come here to-morrow. . . ."

And, to upset her no more, we set off through the turmoil of the streets again and made for the Golden Gate by the wall of the Temple.

Zerah's face was white with fatigue and discomfort. I doubted if she would be able to walk the further two miles. And we had no certainty of Rachel being able to take us in when we got there.

But when I said as much, and suggested trying to find a lodging in the City, she said very earnestly, " No. Let us go to Bethany. He may be there, and there is no rest in the City "— which was true.

We had almost to fight our way through the narrow, crowded streets. For everywhere, in the midst of the flow, there were people standing in bunches, talking and disputing, and from every quarter the country-folk were still pouring into the City, and rambling about seeking their lodgings.

Every now and again would come the clank of steel and the tread of heavy feet all marching as one, as though a mighty giant strode past ; and a Roman patrol would come along, scattering the people as though they were sheep and with no more thought of them. Grim, clean-shaven, hard-faced men they were, with shining helmets and stony eyes that regarded us no more than if we had been actually sheep, or dogs. Our homely folk, in their dusty garments and shrinking ways, made a poor show beside them.

But as soon as Rome had passed they would all bunch together again, chins wagging, and eyes viciously agleam with hate of her, and shining with excitement over the matter that stirred them still more.

And that was Jesus—The Teacher, The Deliverer—The Promised One. Where was he? Had he come? What would he do? What would the High Priest do?

Every group we struggled through, it was the same. Everywhere excited faces and gabbling mouths and eager questionings.

I tried to get news of him from one and another, but learned little. He had not been in the City that day, they all agreed on that. It was said he slept outside for safety.

"And very wise too!" said one. "He'd be wiser still if he went away altogether just now."

"Yes," said another, "Pilate always fears tumults at Passover, and if there is one he'll make The Teacher pay."

No one knew anything definite. It was all hearsay and tittle-tattle, and we pushed on to get away from it all.

We were glad to get out into the country again. We toiled slowly over the lower slopes of the Mount of Olives and so came to Bethany, and sought out Rachel's house.

She was a sharp-featured, energetic little woman, with quick bright eyes. She made no

difficulty about taking us in, since we had brought
our own provisions with us   But her house was
very small, and Zerah had to share her room, and
I to sleep on the floor of the only other room.

We were grateful for that much, for by this
time we were both quite spent, but more by the
discomforts of Jerusalem than by the distance we
had travelled.

CHAPTER XXVIII

OF A REST WITHOUT WHILE THE STORM BREWED WITHIN

BETHANY was very restful after the seething tumult of the City. We were glad we had come.

When we had washed and eaten we went up to the house-top with Rachel, to sit in the cool of the evening. The sun was setting blood-red behind the walls and towers of Jerusalem, which showed black and grim against it; and even at that distance we could hear the low growl of the myriads assembled there.

"It looks like some great crouching monster waiting for its prey," said Zerah depressedly.

"And it sounds like it. I have never seen so many people there, nor in such turmoil," I said.

"Everyone has come this year because of The Teacher," said Rachel. "They say he is to be King and sweep out the Romans."

"That is not his aim," said Zerah quickly.

"The people think it is, but the priests are all against him. If he tries it there will be blood shed."

"He would rather die himself than that,"

said Zerah. " Why can they not understand him ?   He wants only their good."

" They can think of no greater good than to be free of Rome.   It's the one thing their hearts are set on.   And truly they say he went in like a King last Sunday, riding on a foal, just as the old prophets said, and all the people strewing their clothes and palm branches in front of him."

" But that was very strange," said Zerah, gazing at her in amazement.   " And not like him, for he has always set his face against any displays of that kind . . ." and she fell thoughtful.

But Rachel's next words brought her back. " You see," she said, " he had been stopping here in Bethany, with Martha and Mary, as he had done more than once before.   That's their house —the white one next to the mud one.   You heard about Lazarus ? "

" No.   What ? "

" Why, it was the most wonderful thing that ever happened in this world.   Lazarus fell sick. His sisters sent to ask The Teacher to come, hoping he could cure him.   He was a good friend of theirs, you see.   But he delayed, and Lazarus died.   And when The Teacher did at last come, he had been buried four days.   You know what that would mean !   But The Teacher went with them to the tomb and called to him, and Lazarus came back, and he's there to-day alive and well. If you're about you may see him, but everyone stares at him so, and wants to ask him so many questions, that he doesn't go out much in the

daytime yet. But he's often out after nightfall.
. . . And it seems to me, and I suppose to
other people the same, that a man who can bring
folks back from the dead can do pretty much anything he sets his mind to—so why not to being
King and getting rid of Rome ? " she asked
triumphantly.

" That is not the Kingdom he desires," said
Zerah. " He has told them, and told them, and
told them. But they are blind and deaf and
will not understand."

" What is it he wants then ? "

" He wants them to give their hearts to God—
all men, everywhere !—and so to found a New
Kingdom for God on earth. That would be a
bigger Kingdom than Rome and all the rest of
the world put together."

" I'm afraid it's beyond me," said Rachel,
shaking her head. " And I'm sure the people
don't think of it that way."

" If only they would ! " sighed Zerah. " Then
Rome would not trouble them."

" Rome will always trouble everyone that's not
too strong for her."

" God is stronger even than Rome."

The moon had come up over the mountains of
Moab, red and threatening. But as it climbed
the darkening sky it grew smaller and brighter
and flooded the country with silvery light.
It shone white on the City walls and towers and
seemed to whisper " Peace ! " But the City
growled unceasingly.

"There is Lazarus coming out now," said Rachel, in a whisper, and I leaned over the roof to watch him. For a man who had lain dead for four days was, after all, a great wonder.

But Zerah would not move. She said simply, " It is not seemly to stare at him and he does not wish it."

He passed slowly just below us, but his head was covered with his robe, and all I could see as he came towards us was a pallid face and strange deep eyes.

" If he could only tell us about those four days——" I said to Rachel.

" Many have questioned him, but he will not speak of them," she said. " Maybe it is all gone from him. He looks like that."

We were very tired, and Rachel understood and let us get to bed early. And in spite of our anxieties we slept soundly.

CHAPTER XXIX

Of Life and Death at the Prætorium

It seemed to me that I had no more than laid my head down when I was wakened by an insistent thumping on the door.

I got up and opened it. The gray before the dawn was over everything, and there stood Mary's son, John, leaning with both hands on the door-posts, and panting in sobs that almost choked him.

" John ? " I cried, and my heart kicked with apprehension.

He stumbled in and sank down on a stool. His face was as gray as the dawn, and sweat and tears trickled down his face.

" It is all over ! " he gasped.

" Jesus ? "

" They have taken him. . . . They will never let him go alive."

Rachel and Zerah had come in at the sound of him. Zerah's face set like marble as she heard.

" We must go," she whispered. " Where have they taken him, John ? "

" To the house of Caiaphas, on the Mount, near my mother's."

" Let us go ! " she said, and set off without

another word, and when I had gathered up our few belongings, and thanked Rachel, John and I hastened after her.

"Tell us all you know, John," said Zerah, as we hurried along.

"I'll tell you all I saw," said John eagerly. "Jesus and the others ate their supper in our upper room. They sat long over it, and when they came out I was waiting about, hoping to see him again. And oh, Zerah, their faces frightened me—they were so gloomy and anxious looking——"

"Not Jesus!"

"No" . . . he thought for a moment and then said, "His face was not gloomy . . . nor full of fears, like theirs. . . . But it frightened me more than all the others. . . . It was white and set and keen like an eagle's. . . . I never saw him like that before—never! And his eyes were very bright . . . but very sad too. I can't tell you, because I never saw anyone look like that. . . .

"They went towards the Temple, and I followed to see what they were going to do. They went out by the Gate, and down into the valley and over the brook into the garden on Olivet, as he often did. . .

"It was after sunset and I knew the Gate would be closed. Though indeed I could have got in again by Caiaphas's gate on Zion if I'd wanted to, for the gate-keeper is a friend of mine.

"But, you see, I knew from their faces that they

feared something was going to happen, and I
wanted to know what it was.

"So I lay down among the bushes and waited.
And after a long time I saw torches coming across
the valley, and Jesus and his people came down
to meet them. It was some of the Temple
Officers with some soldiers and a lot of rough
fellows.

"When they met I thought there was going to
be a fight. I saw swords out, and I went closer.
But Jesus stopped his people from fighting and
said he was ready to go with them, and they
closed round him and went off. One of the
Temple men saw me and made a grab at me, but
I got away and followed them further off.

"They went round the South wall to Caiaphas's
private gate, and as they were all crowding through
I slipped in too.

"I saw them take him into Annas's house, and
then I ran home to tell my mother, and she said I
should come at once and tell you, for you were the
nearest friends he had."

"Thank you, John dear, for coming so quickly
and for telling us about it," said Zerah, and then,
as if to herself she said with a sob, "Oh, what
will be the end of it ? . . . God forgive them !
God forgive them ! "

Though it was still very early, the City was
evidently all astir. The hoarse growl of it grew
louder with every step we took. More than ever
it sounded like a wild beast hungry for its food.

We passed through the Temple Gate and

thrust into the turmoil of the narrow streets. But we had not now to fight our way. There were no rings and knots of men blocking the passage while they argued and disputed. The crowd was all pushing doggedly the way we wanted to go, and as eager to get there as we were.

There was not much talking. The time for talking was over. Things were happening, though no one seemed to know what.

Broken sentences reached us.

" Yes, in the night—over there on Olivet." . . . " No — no fighting. They say he gave himself up to them." . . . " Caiaphas will make an end of him because of that Temple business." . . . " Yes, it touched his pocket and Old Annas's." . . . " Not what he led us to hope for." . . . " Who *could* understand him ? He had his chance. The people would have risen and followed him anywhere." . . . " Yes, it's all over now. They'll end him one way or another." . . . " A good man . . . wonderful powers, if he'd only known how to turn them to account." . . . " Too soft for the job—a fool, but it's a pity, all the same."

Zerah's white, set face twinged at times as these things smote her. She clung tightly to my arm lest the scuffling crowd should part us.

So we passed by the Temple and were swept along towards Mount Zion, where Annas and Caiaphas lived.

Then suddenly, on some later rumour, the

crowd swerved towards the Prætorium, where Pilate's big house stood among its gardens.

Here there was already a great mass of people standing tense and silent, watching and waiting. Our crowd flowed round its outskirts and pressed in to see what was going on. The ones in front flung over their shoulders such information as they had.

"They've sent him to Pilate." . . . "Yes, inside there." . . . "Pilate hates Caiaphas. He'll thwart him if he can." . . . "He's a bad one to thwart, is Caiaphas"—and much more of the like, all very discomforting to us.

We waited in grievous anxiety and distress.

To these others it was just an unusual happening for Passover Week, and the probable end of the contest between the ancient powers of the Priests and Rulers with this new, surprisingly-gifted Teacher, who had suddenly sprung from nowhere and put them and their vested interests in peril. It was disappointing in view of the hopes they had cherished, but it would be interesting to see which side won.

To us—it was the life of our best-loved friend that hung in the balance. Our hearts were very heavy, and full of prayers for him.

"Now—what's this?"—jerked a tall man behind us, as the dense pack in front began to quiver and sway and thrust back upon itself with cries and snarls and curses.

For through it, cleaving its way like a plow-share, and as regardless of what it cleft, came a

Roman cohort with a centurion at its head, and in its midst—Jesus.

His robe was soiled and torn. His face was white and strained but bravely calm and undaunted, and there were bruises and blood on it. His eyes were wonderful still—sad and pained indeed, but, as John had said, bold and unflinching as an eagle's. They seemed to look past it all to something beyond.

To his guards, he was but one more victim caught in the great machine of the law, of which they were the ruthless instruments. They were hardened to such things.

To the onlookers, he was just a half-broken man being hustled to his doom.

To us, he was, in spite of it all, our Wonderful One, our dearest and best of friends, and this near sight of his suffering chilled the blood in our veins, though the sun was pouring hot on our heads.

" One for Pilate ! " cried the tall man behind us, who seemed to see more than most. " He's a Galilean so Pilate sends him to Herod to judge ! " . . . and then, as an afterthought—" But Herod won't. He has no power in Jerusalem . . . he'll be back again presently. You see if he isn't."

And presently we saw the cohort come plowing back through the crowd, and in the midst was Jesus, clothed now in an old purple robe. But, in spite even of that, his patient dignity was such that the onlookers marvelled and many of them were silent.

Through occasional gaps between the swaying heads in front we caught glimpses of the portico of the Prætorium.

We saw a soldierly figure with a round black head come out and stand at the top of the broad marble steps that led up to the Judgment Hall, and speak to someone below—to Caiaphas, the tall man said. We could not see him. The black-headed soldier, he said, was Pilate, the Procurator.

From those in front, round about Caiaphas, there rose of a sudden, hoarse cries of " Crucify ! Crucify ! "

Zerah's arm clutched mine so tightly that I feared she was about to fall. But it was only the sudden shock of that cruel cry. Her face was like marble, her eyes strained wide in an agony of fear—after her heart, which was with him there in the midst of his enemies.

We saw Pilate stand gazing scornfully down at those below him. He seemed to be arguing with them. Then he raised his hands and shoulders in a gesture of contempt and seemed to call to someone inside. For a soldier came out with a silver basin and a cloth and held it while Pilate washed his hands and dried them.

We did not understand, but the tall man grasped the meaning of it.

" He washes his hands of the matter, and casts the responsibility on the Priests," he said. " So they will have their way with him."

" And that ? " I jerked out.

"They will crucify him; though why, by my life, I cannot see."

And at that Zerah gave a heart-rending sob and sank heavily on my arm. I thought she was about to lose her senses. There was still some water in my bottle, and I hastily gave her a drink, and the tall man behind put his hands under her arms, though, indeed she could not have fallen, so tightly were we packed.

"Shall we go ?—if we can," I whispered into her ear, though I doubted much if it would be possible.

"No—no—no!" she said. "I must see. I must see. . . . Oh, my poor, poor, dear one! What will they do to you ?"

Our neighbours eyed us curiously, but she heeded them not. In all that huge crowd there was but one man concerned her, and though she could not see him the rest were to her as if they were not.

CHAPTER XXX

OF THE WAY OF SORROWFUL TRIUMPH

OF what went on inside there we knew nothing till long afterwards, when Longinus, the centurion, told it all to John.

He told him then with sorrow—for he had by that time come to the truth—how they mocked and maltreated their prisoner. How they set him on a stool for a throne, and twisted a thorn-branch into a crown, and gave him a wand for a sceptre—and then how they scourged him with a leather whip, every thong of which was fanged with iron nails or splinters of bone.

And he told John also that his bearing under it all—his calm dignity, though he was bruised and battered almost to pieces; his patient fortitude when the lash tore pieces out of his flesh; his meekness as they mocked him; and, more than all, the wonder of his anguished eyes, bloodshot with suffering but all unconquerable—it was too much for them.

They were rough and hard and brutal, but they could tell a man when they found one. And they desisted at last because this man was too much for them.

" But," said Longinus, the centurion, to John, " it was months before I got rid of the look of those eyes of his. Wherever I looked they looked back at me. And when I close my eyes now I can see them still."

We waited long under the burning sun, knowing nothing of what was going on inside there. But, after a very long time, the soldiers came out again, and we saw Jesus among them, and two others with him. And then, after another wait, we saw them all move away. The crowd surged after them. We did not know where they were going.

They went up the street that led to the Damascus Gate, and we perforce went with them. And the crowd was very silent now, except some ribald ones whose shouts we could hear in the distance in front. They were probably the hirelings of the High Priest—the ones who had made all the noise in the Courtyard.

When we had got through the gate the crowd spread out and we were able to get along faster.

The soldiers on ahead kept stopping, and before long we caught up with them, and could see Jesus staggering along under a great beam of wood. Zerah's arm shuddered inside mine as she saw it, till it set me shaking too, like one with the palsy.

Suddenly she snatched my water-bottle and darted in among the soldiers.

Jesus had fallen again and lay with his face on the ground. A venomous little Jew, with a most evil face, ran up and began striking him with a stick, till one of the soldiers drove him off with the butt of his spear.

They lifted Jesus up and held the beam off him for a moment. His face was covered with blood and dust, plastered to it by the sweat that streamed from him. The blood was still trickling from the mock crown on his head.

Zerah ran in, pulling off her veil. She sluiced it with water, and wiped the blood and mud off his eyes and face.

In the depth of his woe he knew it to be the act of a friend, and a faint smile of gratitude hovered on his lips.

When he could open his eyes properly, and saw hers, streaming with love and pity, so close to him, his face lighted for a moment with such a look of glad surprise and undying love that even the rough soldiers regarded them with wonder.

When he was speaking of it all with John, long afterwards, Longinus said :

"We took her for a spirit come to comfort him."

And that was what she seemed to many that day. With her long black hair falling about her, and her sweet high face filled with tenderest compassion and untellable love, and in her all the grace of perfect womanhood—yes, it was not surprising that they took her for an angel from heaven come to comfort him.

But their duty had to be done—even though some of them were beginning to feel a distaste for it.

Longinus put her aside, not ungently, and looking about him called a man out of the crowd and bade him carry the beam, and he did it willingly. May the blessing of God rest on him !

Zerah dropped back into the crowd which opened for her to pass. Then she put on her veil and drew it close, and we all moved on again. She was sobbing as if her heart would break. I was in great fear for her, but she would go on.

The soldiers stopped at a great mound, almost a hill, which stands between the road to Samaria, by which we had come into the City the previous day, and the road which leads to Jericho.

The crowd gathered round them, but not very close. Zerah sank down by the roadside and bowed her head between her arms in an agony of grief.

Then after a time we heard the dull blows of the hammers, and she shuddered and writhed.

But I could not look any more than she could. I bowed my head and waited. For him they were doing to death there was dear to the very marrow of our hearts, and every blow was as the stroke of death to us ourselves.

At last from the crowd came a sound like a deep " Oo-oo-ooch "—and we knew that the sufferers were on their crosses.

One wild glance Zerah gave at them and then flung herself down, sobbing as if her heart were broken—great sobs that shook her whole body.

John crouched by us. He had kept close to us all through, saying nothing, but watching everything. Like the rest of us he was confused and confounded by it all. We could none of us understand. It seemed the end of all things. It seemed impossible. Yet there was the cross and our best-beloved was on it.

The crowd began to thin, for from behind the mountains great black clouds came rolling up, and it looked like being a storm.

Round the crosses, some of the High Priest's ruffians hung about jeering and mocking. They looked ready to stone Jesus as he hung there helpless, but the soldiers kept them at a distance.

Some of the other lookers-on joined in their jeers, but by degrees they fell away and few remained but those who loved him.

We heard him cry out more than once in his agony. And each time Zerah quivered as at a blow. And I prayed that he might go quickly. For at times the end is long of coming, on the cross—as long as several days indeed, and the anguish of it no living man may know.

Then suddenly, not far from us, I saw a group of women, bowed with sorrow like ourselves. And I saw that it was Mary, his mother, though her sweet face was so ravaged with her grief that I hardly knew her. And with her were her sister, Clopas's Mary, and some others. They were all weeping bitterly, all broken with their misery and despair.

We heard Jesus cry " Eloi ! Eloi ! " and Zerah shuddered again, for his voice told all his suffering. But my mind flew back to him as a boy standing slim and beautiful on our hill-top, in the dawn and in the storm, with his arms flung up as he cried " Eloi ! Eloi ! " and felt God there.

The sky had grown as black as pitch. A jagged flash of lightning seemed to rip the very heaven above us in twain, and the thunder-clap that came at the same moment was so close and so terrific that it beat the breath out of us.

We lay cowering, while above us, and over the City, the lightning shot and stabbed venomously, and the thunder crashed and rattled as if it would shake it to pieces.

Many, I am sure, that day thought it was the anger of God for the deed that had been done.

We dared not move. And as we lay there, pressed to the earth, with death crashing all about us, and the fear of it in most of our hearts, there came a sudden lull in the storm, and that strange silence was more awful than the terror before had been.

But as we lay, in great fear and misery, there came a cry from the cross—a strange, loud, triumphant cry, " It is finished . . . Father, receive my spirit ! "

Clear, on that great silence, it came to us. Clear it seemed to ring out over the darkened City, and out and on over all the earth. And so it has rung in my ears ever since, and does so to this day.

" He is dead," whispered John.

" Thank God ! " I said, thinking only that his suffering was ended.

We waited still. We waited long. But though
the other two writhed miserably on their crosses,
Jesus moved no more. And our sick hearts found
a little comfort in the certainty that he suffered
no longer.

" Take me home, Azor," said Zerah at last.
" I am spent "—and indeed she looked it—her
face white and set like a piece of ivory, her great
dark eyes lustreless, lost in hollow pools of misery
and pain.

" To our house," said John. " My mother
would wish it so. She has never ceased to chide
herself for not being able to take you in yesterday."

" Yesterday ? " said Zerah confusedly.

And to me also it seemed impossible. Was it
only yesterday that we trod this same road and
passed under that same gate into the City ?

Only yesterday ? . . . We had lived a lifetime
since yesterday—a life-time—and a death-time !
And out of our lives had gone what life could
never give us back if we lived to be as old as the
ancients. We felt old and worn and bereft—
as Zerah said—spent.

It was dark as night still as we went slowly and
heavily back into the City. And there the
narrow streets were like tombs, and those who
passed were like spirits come out of them.

Mary welcomed us contritely, though there was
no reason for her feeling so.

When she heard that Jesus was dead she
drew her veil over her face and gave way to her
grief.

John would have had us eat, but Zerah shook her head.

" All I want is to sleep, John," she said wearily—and to herself—" to sleep . . . and sleep . . . and never to awake ! " and he took her away to the guest-chamber.

CHAPTER XXXI

OF THE BARING OF ZERAH'S HEART

FROM the time she lay down, and all through the following day, which was the Sabbath, Zerah slept like one dead, and Mary was growing desperately anxious about her.

She had had nothing to eat for over forty hours. We began to fear she would slip away from us in her sleep, as she herself, I knew, would wish. Still, unless she died for lack of food, sleep was the very best thing for her. Body, mind, and soul, she had been tried beyond endurance, and spent energies crave above all things rest and time for recovery.

Several times during that long day, Mary, in her anxiety about her, drew me into the room to reassure herself that she was still alive. And, but for the slow and hardly-to-be-discerned movement of her breathing, we might indeed have thought her dead.

She lay like a beautiful marble statue. The pain and sorrow had left her face and it was as it used to be, calm and sweet and wondrous fair to look upon.

It was close on sunset when, as we stood watching her, her eyelids fluttered and her large dark eyes looked wonderingly up at us. Then she sat up, still staring at us, and asked eagerly, " Where is he ? "

" Who, Zerah ? "

" Jesus "—and she seemed surprised at my asking such a question.

" Jesus. . . ." I faltered, taken all aback.

" Yes "—with a small, provoked knitting of the brow at my stupidity.

" He has been here," she said, insistently. " Where is he gone ? "

" But . . . Zerah . . . you know . . . our friend has . . . has gone from us——"

" Gone ? "—she drew her hand across her brow, slowly and thoughtfully. " Ah . . . I remember. . . . But he is not dead, as you think, Azor——"

And I feared for her reason. But her eyes were quite steady, and clear and bright as ever, and in them were the little shining stars, like those that were always in the eyes of him we loved.

" I am very hungry," she said. " Will you get me to eat, Mary dear ? " and Mary, who had stood wondering, hasted to get her food.

" And when we have eaten, Azor, I want to go home to Nazaret," said Zerah, while she was away.

" But—can you, Zerah ?—Are you fit for the journey yet ? "

" Fit for it ?—Why not ? " she asked in surprise. " I came all right, did I not ? "

" Yes, truly, you came all right. But . . . we have been sorely tried since then."

" When I have eaten I shall be ready. . . . We shall walk better under the moon than under the sun, and I would be out of Jerusalem. . . . It was cruel to my Beloved. . . . We could get as far as Beth-El and pass the Sabbath there."

" But this is the Sabbath."

" This—is—the—Sabbath ? "—she gazed at me doubtfully.

" You slept all through the night and all through the day."

" Ah ! " she said, wonderingly. " Then that is why I am so hungry, and why I feel so ready to walk now. . . . Then the Sabbath is over and we can go."

Mary came in with food for her, and she ate hungrily.

But when I told her of Zerah's wish to start for home at once, she was very much against it. She spoke of robbers and wild beasts that prowled by night, but it was all of no avail. Zerah was set on getting home and she made light of Mary's fears.

" No robbers would look twice at us," she said, " and as to wild beasts we will not fear them."

She was set on it, and so when we had both eaten we bade Mary farewell, and John came a little of the way with us.

As we issued from the City gate our eyes fell at once on the mound beyond, on which the crosses stood.

Zerah stopped and gazed at them with wide, wondering eyes.

" They have taken him away," she said softly. " Oh, I wonder where they have laid him ! "— and she hesitated as though she would fain turn and make enquiry. But, after stopping so for a moment, she fell on her knees, and then rose and went on.

When it came time for John to turn back he was very loth to go.

" I would I were going with you to Nazaret," he said wistfully. " I never did like Jerusalem, but now I hate it. . . ."

" I know," said Zerah softly, in a voice that showed she understood. " But you and your mother will soon be coming up to us, John——"

" Nothing will ever be quite the same," he said dolefully.

" No," she said, very gently. " Nothing will ever be quite the same again—not quite the same. . . . The sun has gone down but he will rise again. And we can walk by the light of the moon . . . and the stars . . ."—and perhaps she was thinking, as it made me think, of the stars that shone always in the eyes of our beloved.

And when we had insisted on him going no further, and had bidden him farewell, we walked on along the road that wound among the rough brown hills and climbed steadily towards Beth-El.

It was then, as we walked side by side under the white Paschal moon, that she bared her soul to me.

I had always loved her—as I have told before—

with a love which held her in highest reverence—
as one apart, above, almost as one who belonged
of right to another world. It was quite different
from my love for Zoe, who filled my heart completely and yet left room in it for this pure
adoration of her sister.

I worshipped her and she knew it, and blessed
me with a very warm affection in return.

And, after what we had gone through together,
it was natural that she should open her heart and
speak freely to the one in the whole world who
could best understand and enter wholeheartedly
into all her feelings in the matter.

"Azor, my brother," she said softly, as we
walked along our shadows in the bright moonlight,
"you believed my mind was wandering when I
said Jesus had been there while I slept."

"Yes, Zerah."

"Perhaps it was a dream," she said. "But to
me it was very real. He stood by my bedside,
and said, 'I am not dead, beloved. Go home
to Nazaret and wait there till I come.'"

"It has made you happier even to dream it."

"If it was a dream!"—and then she spoke
strange sweet things, as a prophetess of old might
have done—things that at that time were a little
beyond me.

"They think they have killed him on the cross,
Azor. But you can't kill Love even on a cross.
. . . And he was Love. . . . He was The
Very Love of God. Love never dies and so he is
not dead. . . . The—Very—Love—of—God!

. . . How—I cannot tell you, because you and I are only human. Our minds are not able to comprehend it, but at times in our souls we may get glimpses of it. And sometime we shall understand it all."

She was silent for a time and we pressed steadily on.

Then she began again abruptly—" It was that night he and I went up the hill together . . . you remember ? "

" Yes."

" I knew that he loved me. A woman always knows. And for me—I loved him with my whole heart and soul, and I longed to let him know it.

" We went up hand in hand, and the great love in his heart pulsed through from his soul to mine and from mine to his. We did not speak one word all the way up. Words are but poor things when soul can speak to soul without them.

" He led me to his favourite place, and we sat looking out over the great plain all white in the moonlight.

" And then, after a time, he said, ' Zerah, beloved, you know that I love you. I love you as, of a surety, man never before loved woman,'— and my heart sang for joy, and I needs must show it. But when I would have put my arms round his neck and drawn him to me, he gently restrained me.

" And then, very lovingly and tenderly, he told me about himself—how that, ever since he grew out of childhood and was able to think things out

for himself—and he spoke very gladly and grate-
fully of all that his father, Joseph, had been to
him—and had done for him,—all that time there
had been growing in him a feeling which became
a certainty, that God wanted him for some very
special work—and wanted him wholly.

" Whatever it was, that work was to be supreme
in his life. It was to be his life-work. He did
not yet know fully what it was, except that it
was to be for the good of his fellows, but God had
chosen him for it and he had answered the call.

" There was no shadow of doubt in his heart
and mind about it. He knew it meant sacrifice.
It might mean the sacrifice of everything—of life
itself. And he was prepared for that—everything—to the uttermost—and beyond. He had
given himself wholly to whatever God might ask
of him.

" And with deep reverence he told me how God
had communed with him there, on that hill-top—
not once, but many times—and had instructed
him as to the work He would have him do, and
how to set about it.

" He said the sin and sorrow and suffering of
the world lay heavy on God's heart. For it was
His world and He felt as a father towards it.

" But it had wandered away from Him and He
longed for it back. And it was to be Jesus's
work to call it back and show it the way.

" God gave him wonderful powers—we know
that, Azor, for we have seen him use them—
and always for other people's good.

" And God told him that he was His own Son
—His dear and only Son—and that all power was
to be his—all power on earth and in heaven."

For the first time since she began, I spoke.

" Zerah, dear," I said, " it is very wonderful,
but I don't think I can understand it. I know
he himself told us something like that, but. . . ."

" It is beyond our understanding, Azor. . . .
But you have known him—better than most, and
you would believe anything he told you."

" Everything," I said earnestly.

" And so you will believe this of him, even as
I do."

We paced along in silence again—she, full of
her gracious memories—I, pondering deeply, but
very confusedly, all she had said. For, as I had
told her, it was all far beyond me, and I felt like
a man groping blindly in a morning mist, when
the unseen sun up above fills it with a light that
makes one's head spin.

" He told me," she began again after a time,
" that his heart had gone out to me that very
first day when he came down the hill to welcome
us after our journey. . . .

" And how he had fought against it, as God's
call grew clearer and clearer to him.

" ' Beloved,' he said to me, ' you will never
know what I have suffered for your dear
sake. . . .' "

" But," she broke out eagerly again, " Azor—
that other day when he hung there on the cross,
I came to understand a little of what one may

suffer for love's sake. My heart was with him there, crucified with him there. When at last it broke I learned a little of what he had suffered for me. I began to understand. . . . Love is greater than Life or Death and nothing can kill it. . . . Nothing. . . . Nothing. . . . Nothing ! "

And presently she began again where she had broken off. "He said, 'Beloved, I loved you with my whole being. But my Father's will had to be supreme, and for long I strove to reconcile my love and longing for you with my love and duty to Him. I have lain whole nights before Him up here, pleading with Him in agony, for you had become a very part of my heart and my life; to give you up felt like tearing my heart to pieces.

" ' But, very lovingly and tenderly, He showed me that it could not be. He had told me from the first that His Way meant sacrifice. He showed me that if I was to help Him to save the world I must be ready to give up everything . . . everything.

" ' But He showed me, too, that in the end the joy would exceed the pain—that the saving of the world was greater than anything and everything in the world—was greater than the world itself. He was very gentle with me,' he said. 'Very tender and long-suffering. For He is Love, and He understands.'

" My heart was very sore. It yearned and bled for him; but I saw, though only dimly then, through the pain of it, that what I had hoped for us could never be. I felt all the glory and the joy of his love—and—ah me!—all the pain!

"I prayed to God to help me to bear it, and I felt uplifted beyond earth and all mortal desires. . . . . Nay, not all. For still I was a woman and it was as a woman that I loved him, —beyond myself and every earthly thing.

"I said to him, 'I love you, heart and soul and body. I will try to understand. Kiss me once, Beloved—my life, my soul—as a bridegroom kisses his bride, and it shall suffice me!'

"He gazed at me, Azor, with all the love of his great heart in his eyes. He bent towards me. And, knowing now what I did, I came nigh to swooning with the thought of it all.

"I closed my eyes to receive that last kiss which was to be the crown and consecration of our love, and my whole being went out to meet it.

"But it did not come, and when at last I looked up at him his face was gray and tight with pain, and he was no longer gazing at me but up into the sky as if he communed with someone there.

"And then—abruptly, but oh, so gently—he put me from him, and I sank down in a heap, feeling like to die and very wishful to.

"He placed his hands on my head and very tenderly begged God's blessing and comfort for me . . . . and I felt new strength and grace flow into me at his touch.

"Then he turned and passed out of my sight

into the darkness of the trees. And when I was myself again I went down home alone. My heart was very sore and yet I felt within me a joy no words can tell."

"Alone! Alone!" she said, half to herself. "But never alone again. For his love has always been warm about me and always will be . . . . always! . . . . always!"

I told her how I had gone up the hill next day at noon, when his mother grew anxious about him. And how I had found him lying there prone, with his head sunk down between his arms as though he had spent himself in prayer and fallen asleep praying. And how, when at last he woke up, he raised his arms again, and cried "Eloi! Eloi!"

"As he did on the cross," she said quickly.

"As he did on the cross. He cried to his Father."

And in the light of all she had told me I knew now that he had fought a great battle with himself that night up there—such a fight as mortal man had never known, and had won it. But he had suffered—oh, he had suffered. I had seen that at the time.

We had both of us much to think of, and we went on in silence till we came to the little inn at Beth-El, where we were to lodge for the night.

CHAPTER XXXII

Of the Wonderful Visit

I DID not sleep much that night, for my mind was over-full with all that Zerah had spoken of. I was like a man after too big a meal. It needed time to digest.

We were early on the road. As we started, the sun looked silently, wonderingly, over the mountains of Ammon, as though doubtful of what he might see after that dread yesterday. Then, as though satisfied, he soared up boldly and joyously and climbed the thin blue sky.

The hills of Ephraim on our left shone golden for a space, and far away on the right the peak of Nebo showed still his shadowed side. The air was sweet and crisp, but very still.

I was, I suppose, over-wrought by all that had happened, and strung tense. For indeed it seemed to me that that great stillness was full of expectation—as though the very earth were holding its breath for something to happen. And Zerah, I think, felt it too, for she kept looking earnestly about her and above her with wide wondering eyes. But her one desire seemed to be to get home without a moment's loss of time and we walked quickly, and for a time in a silence in keeping with all about us.

But at last I had to try to get some more light on the thoughts which were churning in my mind. And so instant were they to me that I spoke as though no night had interrupted our previous talk.

" Zerah," I said, " who then do you really believe Jesus to be ? "

And instantly she answered, " The Son of the Most High—His Best Beloved—His Only One ! . . . Did he not tell us so himself that day on the hill by Gilboa ? "

" Yes—I know. . . . But . . . it is beyond me. I cannot comprehend it," I said dazedly, for by the way she said it I saw that she herself believed it beyond all doubt. " You see, I cannot forget that he worked with me at the bench——"

" Never forget that, Azor. It shall come to be your greatest glory," she said vehemently.

" Do you understand it all yourself ? " I persisted.

" No. But I believe him because he told me himself—and I love him. That is better even than understanding. Who am I that I should understand God and His wonderful ways ? "

We walked for a time in silence and then I asked again :

" I am stupid, I know, Zerah. Perhaps it is because I couldn't sleep all night for thinking of it all. But . . . if he died on the cross, how can he help to save the world and do all that God wanted him to do ? "

" It was only his body they could crucify," she said earnestly. " He himself—all that was really him, and all that he means—is alive still. I am sure of it. I know it. I feel it. And he will go on doing the work God gave him to do till it is all completed."

I could only shake my head uncomprehendingly. She took it for doubt or disbelief.

" You do not doubt his own word, Azor ? " she asked sharply.

" It is not that—only I can't understand it."

" Some day we shall understand. But it may not be in this life. Until then, trust his word as I do."

And presently she broke out again, in that strange uplifted way of hers which always made me think of the prophetesses of old, " Don't you see how wonderful it all is, Azor ? Why, it is the most wonderful thing that has happened since the world was made. . . ."

" What is, Zerah ? " I asked, much mystified, for she sometimes just spoke aloud the thoughts that were running in her head, and it was not always easy to follow her.

" His dying like that—on the cross. Think of it ! God's own Son giving up everything he could give—his own life—in trying to turn the world from its evil ways—the world that God Himself made. . . . God's Son crucified by God's own creatures ! . . . It's almost un-thinkable ! "

" But," I said, " I still don't see how his being

crucified is going to turn the world from its evil ways."

"People will never forget it—or him. Never! It will grow and grow upon them—all his goodness and all he did for them ; and then—the cross! . . . No, they cannot ever forget him, no matter how they try to."

I shook my head still. The eyes of my understanding were not yet open even as much as hers were. Once again I said, "It is all very wonderful. But I cannot understand it yet."

"It's beyond us. But I feel it though I can't understand it. . . ." And then, following out her own deep thoughts again, "The Law says that by the shedding of blood comes atonement and remission of sin. . . . Like the goat in the wilderness when Aaron laid on him the sins of the people. . . . He was like that . . ." and she went silent again, but her face was full of light.

It was towards nightfall when we drew near that crucifix of Bargas, thief and murderer, in the neighbourhood of Jacob's Well. Gerizim rose darkly between us and the yellow evening sky. The top of Ebal still caught the rays of the setting sun, but the shadows were chasing them swiftly upwards. The cross stood grim and stark, and I feared the sight of it would recall her sorrow.

But, to my exceeding surprise, she stood quietly and gazed at it, and then fell on her knees.

And when she rose, she said quietly :

"Never again will I despise a cross, for it will always remind me of my Beloved. And on every cross I shall see only him. . . . Oh, my dear one! my dear one!" and we went in silence.

We reached home on the evening of the third day, and received a thankful welcome from Zoe and the boys and my mother.

They were shocked and saddened by our telling of all that had happened, and we were a very silent family that night.

But both Zoe and my mother, I could see, were quietly amazed at Zerah's bearing.

"What is it, Azor?" asked Zoe, when we were alone together. "Does she not feel it? I should have thought it would have broken her heart."

And I tried my best to explain what was in Zerah, but made but a poor hand at it, and Zoe still wondered greatly.

Zerah took up her household duties next day as bravely as ever, and I set to work on some jobs that awaited me. My mind and heart were very full and still very dazed, but the handling of my tools again was a great help to me and tended to settle my thoughts.

In the evening we were all sitting in the workshop as the sun went down, when Zerah quietly laid aside her distaff and spindle and went out, and we saw her going quickly up the hill.

"Now where is she going?" said Zoe, jumping up as though she would call to her or run after her.

"Let her alone, Zoe," I said. "She understands more of it all than we do. It will be good for her to be up there."

And we sat on in the fading light, and I told them more of what we had seen in Jerusalem. My mother asked earnestly if we had seen Jesus's mother, and was very sorrowful as I told them about her.

And then . . . it had grown almost dark. . . . I scarce know how to tell it, and even now I would not venture, but, that others, whose word weighs more than mine, had the same experience. . . .

In the strange half-light we saw Zerah coming down the hill again, and one with her. And, trotting by their side, with quick, loving up-glances, was a little brown dog whom I had loved but had never expected to see again.

And when they drew near, Zoe jumped up with a wild look at me and whispered :

" It is Jesus ! And you said he was dead ! "

I could not speak. I stood as one bereft.

They came in to us and he sat down just where he used to sit, by the bench. And Tobias, after a friendly word with each of us, to which we were too amazed to respond properly, immediately set himself to the discovery of his old friend the mouse ; but, though he nosed and rooted with great energy, he did not succeed in finding him.

And Jesus talked with us quietly and happily, but he did not touch any of us. That was the only thing that made it different from the many times he had sat there before. Azor and Zadok were with us and gazed at him wonderingly. In the former times he would have had one on each knee and their arms about his neck.

No, I cannot tell you much of what he said to us, for I was quite dazed and my wits were more astray than ever.

But I know that when he came in he said gently, " Peace be with you all ! " and he bade us not be afraid, for it was he himself. And when my eyes strayed instinctively to his hands and his feet I knew that it really was so. But he knew my thought and said, with his own sweet smile, " Yes, Azor—but Zerah did not need to look at them ! " and he looked lovingly at her, and she at him with worshipful adoration.

Then he asked my mother for one of her cakes, and tremblingly she went into the house and brought him one. And he broke it, saying, " In the breaking of bread give thanks and hold me always in remembrance ! " and he gave to each of us, and ate of it himself, and gave a little bit to Tobias.

And as I gazed at him in very great amazement, he knew again all that was whirling in my head, and he said—" Not yet can you understand, my Azor "—and o,h how my heart leaped at the old friendly words. " Accept me in faith. And believe—as Zerah does ! "

And he said, " And this is what I would have you believe—that I am Love—the Love that is God. For this I came—to bring to the world His Spirit of Love and Peace and Truth. And that I leave with you that you and all men may

be one with Us—My Father . . . Your Father!
. . . The misguided ones could kill my body,
but they could not kill God's Love . . . Love God
and serve Him! Love your neighbour and
serve him! Think as you know I would have you
think! And in all things try to do as I would
have you do! . . . And may the blessing of
The Most High be upon you all, now and
always!"

He sat for a while among us, and there were
other things he said. But those are the ones I
recall. And, indeed, I wonder that I can recall
anything at all, seeing the state of mind I was in.

Then, raising his hands in benediction, he
looked lovingly upon us with the star-shine in his
eyes. And oh, the wonder of him!—so calm and
sweet and lofty—so graciously dignified!

My mind flew back to him as we had seen him
last—staggering under his beam, blinded with
sweat and dust and blood, drooping broken on
his cross. And now——!

A great calm fell on my heart—a great peace
and assurance. For here he stood before us—
Conqueror!—Supreme!—and yet our best
beloved friend and brother!

Then he went quietly out of the door towards
the hill. But when we looked to see him and his
little friend on the path which led upwards, they
came not, and we saw them no more.

CHAPTER XXXIII

Of the Long Days since

JOHN and his mother, Mary, arrived a week later, and they were bursting with their wonderful news. They could not get past our house to go to their own, but came in and sat and poured it all out for a full hour.

"Jesus is not dead," said John excitedly, "though we saw him die on the cross; and Longinus is certain he was dead; and old Joseph of Arimathea, who lives near us, buried him in his new tomb in his garden; and they sealed it and set a guard over it. And the soldiers never slept, though Caiaphas has given them money to say they did and that Jesus's followers stole his body —Roman soldiers and Longinus in charge of them!—Think of it!

"Longinus says that while they watched—it was early Sabbath morning—the earth shook, and the great stone in front of the tomb rolled heavily back, breaking all the seals; and a flaming white spirit sat on the stone, and they were frightened almost out of their senses. They stood and watched but dared not go near.

"Then Jesus's Mother, Joseph's Mary, and the

other women came with spices to lay upon his
body, and the angel told them he was not there,
and that they were to go and tell Peter and the
others—that's Simon, you know. But they call
him Peter now. And Peter came running, and
he found it was all true, though he hadn't believed
it.

" And afterwards all Jesus's followers gathered
in that upper room in our house, where they
supped with him that other night—all except one."
. . . And he hesitated a moment as though to
say more about that, and then went on, " And
they locked the door for fear of Caiaphas and his
people. But, although the door was locked, Jesus
came in among them and talked with them.

" Peter himself told me all about it. I like
Peter. And many others have seen Jesus and
talked with him. It's almost past believing.
What do you make of it, Azor ? "

" He has been here too, John."

" Jesus ?—here ?—How ?—When ? "

We told them, and what Jesus had said to us ;
and he and his mother were stricken silent and
could only stare dumbly at us.

" But what does it all mean, Azor ? " asked
John's mother tremulously, when she found her
speech again.

" It means that Jesus, who worked with me at
this bench, and was so dear a friend to us all, is in
very truth the Son of the Most High—the
Eternal—the Son of God."

" The Son of God ! " and she gazed at me

dazedly. " The — Son — of — God !   No "—
shaking her head, " I cannot understand it."

" It is too wonderful for any of us to understand, Mary. But he told us so himself, and we
believe it because we know him and love him."

" Do you understand it, Zerah ? " Mary
asked, turning helplessly to her.

" I don't understand, Mary, but I know,"
said Zerah earnestly. " My heart and my mind
and my spirit all tell me it is true. For I have
known and loved him, and he told me so himself,
and I can trust him."

.   .   .   .   .   .

Long afterwards Peter and John—who was then
also known as Marcus, or Mark—made a book
about Jesus and all they remembered of what
he said and did.

But long before that, and ever since he left us,
we treasured every thought of him and talked
often of him as we sat in the evening light. And
as far as we could we have lived as he told us to do,
thinking as we believe he would have thought,
and serving our neighbours as he would have us,
and so serving God.

Zerah was very wonderful. She never mourned
—as well she might—over the loss of one who had
been so dear to her. She went about her work
with a face of calm but joyous expectation, as
though she might see him again at any moment.
And she gave herself without stint to the necessi-
ties of all about her.

There were few in Nazaret, or in all that district,

who did not at one time or another rejoice in her service.

The women got into the way of coming up continually to ask her advice in all their many troubles, or if they could not come themselves sent one of the children to beg her to come to them. She never denied herself to any, and never a house she entered but was instantly the brighter and happier for her presence.

For the very look of her sweet, loving face drew their hearts to her' as the sun draws the flowers. And she straightened out all their troubles, and tended all their needs, with a gentle grace that almost made them feel as if they were doing her a favour by giving her the opportunity of helping them. The sick, the poor, all little children, and all suffering animals appealed to her especially, and none ever lacked aught that she could give.

And she never seems to grow any older. For the spirit that is in her, and that joyous expectation of her soul, seem to keep her as young and fair as when she last set eyes on him she loved above herself and all earthly things.

After his death on the cross we never, save that once, saw our dearly-loved friend again. But we have never felt him lost to us, nor very far away.

Very often indeed he seems so close to us that we still at times turn to speak to him, and only then come to ourselves and remember.

But if he is not there in the body we feel him there in the spirit, and spirit speaks to spirit without the need of words.

So we live in the constant hope of seeing him again sometime; if not here then in the larger life to which he has gone on before us. And that feeling has lifted from us entirely all that fear of death which, we know, lies like a heavy weight on some folks all their lives.

We are contented and happy here. We have perhaps more than most to be thankful for. For we feel assured that when this life ends what comes after will be infinitely· better. For there we shall meet again him whom we so much loved, and who so loved us and all his fellows.

.   .   .   .   .   .

Now all these things I have set down here that my children, and their children, and their children's children may know that as a boy and as a man I knew Jesus and loved him as my dearest friend. And that same Jesus, who played with me on the hills, and worked with me in his father's workshop at Nazaret, was in truth The Christ, the Son of the Most High God.